ONCE A SCOUNDREL . . .

To Bob Grantham, marriage was no barrier to a full and widely broadcast sex life.

''Is that why you divorced?'' the special agents asked Grantham's ex-wife.

''One of the reasons. The biggest one, I guess you could say. I don't want you to think I didn't try. But all those women . . . and the times he'd just up and disappear . . . ''

''Pardon me? You say he has been known to disappear before this?''

''Oh, I know what you're thinking,'' Jacquelyn O'Hara said. ''But I can tell you, this is different. His dogs, see. Bob would never go off and leave his dogs. That just isn't like him. No, this time it's real.''

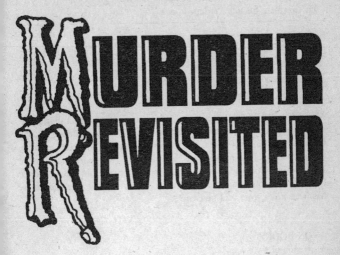

MURDER REVISITED

STEVE BRADY AND FRANK RODERUS

AVON BOOKS ◆ NEW YORK

MURDER REVISITED is a journalistic account of an actual murder investigation and the events surrounding the 1987 disappearance of Bob Grantham in Tampa, Florida. The events recounted in this book are true, although some of the names have been changed. The scenes and dialogue have been reconstructed based on tape-recorded formal interviews, police department records, and published news stories. Quoted court testimony has been taken from trial transcripts.

AVON BOOKS
A division of
The Hearst Corporation
1350 Avenue of the Americas
New York, New York 10019

1

Blood!—so much blood—old and dried, a rich, dark, velvety chocolate color against the white of the upholstery. But it was blood—there was no doubt about that.

Manny Pondakos's pace slowed and, almost involuntarily, his expression froze into a calculatedly neutral display. While he sauntered on, seemingly unconcerned, toward the older model Thunderbird, his eyes swept left, right, left again, although without any outward display of the intense vigilance that now held him.

When there was that much blood, there was—or had been—at least that much trouble.

Pondakos hesitated, carefully sweeping the immediate area. Searching for . . . anything—anything out of the ordinary. Looking for watchers—anyone who might be keeping this blood-soaked automobile under surveillance. There was no one that he could see. If anyone was interested in the Thunderbird, they were too good to be spotted this easily.

All Manny Pondakos could see around the Thunderbird were more cars, dozens of them lined up in the gray half-light of the parking area at Tampa International Airport. The car that interested Pondakos—no, more than interested, the car that *commanded* his attention—was in section B2. It was nosed into the parking bay like a pig to the trough.

As he crossed the dark asphalt driveway and approached the side of the car from behind habit took over, superseding reason, and Pondakos shifted his carry-on flight bag from his right hand to his left.

Not that there would be any cause for him to reach for a weapon. Reason told him that. He made the shift, anyway.

While his face was still expressionless and neutral, Manny Pondakos took one more slow look around, then bent to examine the interior of the auto more closely.

That first, distant glimpse hadn't begun to tell the story here.

The white leather upholstery was smeared thick with blood, so much so that it looked like crudely applied barn paint, thick and clotted over the surfaces of the passenger seat, coating the passenger side headrest, spattered onto the right front door, on the floor, even some on the dashboard.

A newspaper had been spread open on the front seat in a hasty, careless attempt to hide the evidence of the blood. Around the edges of the newspaper were swirls and smears that indicated someone may even have tried to clean up some of the mess. If this was what was left after a cleanup attempt had been made, then. . . .

Pondakos straightened up, took one more long, searching look around the scene and gave his attention this time to the car itself. It was an older model Ford Thunderbird, one of the big, gunboat-size models predating the time when all automobiles began looking like oversized throat lozenges. The exterior of the car was blue with a white top; the interior was also white—or had been. The car had a Florida tag from Polk County, a large county immediately east of Hillsborough County, where Tampa and the airport were located.

The car had been sitting idle in the airport parking lot

for some time. That was easily seen by the film of dust that had accumulated on the windshield and other glass surfaces. Manny Pondakos was not expert enough to be able to judge how long the Thunderbird had been here, but he could easily reckon that it had been a matter of days, possibly weeks.

Fortunately, he knew there were ways to find out precisely when the car had been parked here. But that would have to wait just a bit longer.

Before doing anything else, Pondakos made his way to the back of the Thunderbird and bent low. Stale dust tickled his nose and he fought back an impulse to sneeze, then leaned closer and slowly, deliberately, drew a long breath in through his nose.

There was, mercifully, no sickly sweet stench of decay emanating from the closed trunk. In all probability, then, there was no corpse inside.

That was perhaps his first thought, of course, because in Manny Pondakos's opinion no one living person—or any other creature small enough to have been in the front seat of the car—could have suffered the loss of that much blood and remained alive.

Straightening with a contained but heartfelt sigh of relief, Manny Pondakos took another slow, careful look around.

Then in long, purposeful strides he started off in the direction of the airport terminal.

2

The marked patrol car belonging to the Tampa International Airport Police Department came to a stop at the curb and the uniformed officer leaned across the seat to speak to a man in a conservative business suit who was standing there. "Are you the person who called in?" the officer asked.

"That's right. Special Agent Supervisor Manny Pondakos with the Florida Department of Law Enforcement." Pondakos showed the officer his ID. "Mind if I get in?"

"No, I suppose not. My dispatcher said you have a problem?" It was definitely more of a question than a comment.

"Not me. All I have is a plane to catch. But I think you have a situation in B2 that needs to be looked at. The reason I wanted to meet your car here is that it will be easier to show you where it is than give directions secondhand."

After Pondakos got in the car, the TIA patrolman nodded and put his car in gear. "My name is Houck, by the way. Officer James Houck."

"Pleased to meet you, Officer Houck," Pondakos said formally. "Turn here. That's it." It occurred to him that

Houck would quite certainly know the way to Section B2 without being told.

"You say you're in a hurry to catch a plane?" Houck asked.

Pondakos nodded. "I'm assigned to the Tampa office, but this afternoon I'm supposed to be in Fort Lauderdale giving a lecture for the Broward County Sheriff's Office. I'll still have time to make my flight if this doesn't take too long."

"We'll try to see that you make your plane," Houck volunteered.

"Over there in the next aisle. See the blue and white Thunderbird next to the Buick? That's the one we want."

"All right." Houck made the turn and stopped immediately behind the Ford.

He went to the side of the car and looked in, then whistled softly. "Is that—?"

"Blood. Right."

"Are you sure? It doesn't look like . . . I mean . . . you know."

"It isn't bright red and shiny. But it's blood all right. I spent five years in Homicide with the Pinellas County Sheriff's Office, Houck. Believe me, I've seen more blood than I ever wanted to. Old and new. This is the real stuff."

"But . . . there's so *much* of it," Houck protested, unwilling to accept the implications of that statement.

"Yes. Isn't there?" SAS Pondakos glanced at his watch but didn't attempt to hurry Houck. He still had ample time to make his flight. And if he missed the plane and therefore the lecture too, well, you do whatever duty requires, regardless of personal preferences. Still, he thought he should be able to make it in time.

"How'd you find it?" Houck asked.

"Just walking by, as a matter of fact. I'm parked over there," he pointed, "and this is the shortest way to the terminal. I saw the blood when I was still fifty, sixty feet away. Took a quick look inside and went to find a telephone so I could notify your people. It's as simple as that.''

Houck frowned and shook his head. "This sort of thing, if it's what I think it must be . . . we generally worry about little stuff. You know—parking tickets, abandoned cars, the odd break-in. But nothing like . . . this.'' He looked inside the Thunderbird again and made a sour face.

The Tampa International Airport Authority operated its own independent police department of fifty-four sworn officers plus supporting personnel. But like Houck told the Florida Department of Law Enforcement supervisor, a major crime was beyond the scope of their everyday activity.

If, that is, a crime had been committed here, which still had yet to be determined.

"Do you need me for anything else, Houck?''

"No, I suppose not.'' Officer Houck was still having difficulty accepting the many possible implications—very few of which were innocent—of what he was seeing inside that Thunderbird.

SAS Pondakos gave Houck a business card. "If you need me for anything. . . .''

"Sure. Thanks.'' Houck added a rueful smile and said, ''I think.''

Pondakos nodded in understanding, then headed briskly toward the busy airport terminal to catch his commuter flight to Fort Lauderdale. He was already thinking about the lecture he would be delivering that afternoon, talking about the Florida Racketeer Influenced and Corrupt Organization (RICO) Act and how investigators could make use of it to close down continuing crime operations that otherwise might squeeze through loopholes.

* * *

"Tampa, this is one-oh-eight." Houck released the key on his radio mike. He had to wait only a moment for the response.

"One-oh-eight, Tampa."

"I need a supervisor in Section B2," Houck reported. "Also you better call the FDLE and see if they can send a crime-scene crew out here from the lab." Like most small police agencies the TIA department made no attempt to maintain their own exacting—and expensive—crime laboratory, instead relying on the expert services of the Florida Department of Law Enforcement.

"What do you have there, one-oh-eight—a burglary?"

"Negative. Possibly something serious, but I can't be sure yet. I'll tell you about it when I get in."

"Ten-four, one-oh-eight. I'll have the sergeant on his way in a minute, then bring the FDLE in for you."

"After you do that, Tampa, I'd like a license check on Florida tag 976HFB."

"Ten-four."

TIA police sergeant Dan Raley arrived within minutes and was quickly briefed by Houck. There was little the two officers could do, though, until the crime lab truck arrived with the technicians and the equipment to begin collecting physical evidence from the scene. It had not yet been determined that this was, in fact, a crime scene, but no chances could be taken. Courts of law quite literally have years in which to decide what should or should not have been done at a crime scene, and field officers have learned that wariness is a virtue.

While Houck and Raley were waiting in Houck's car the radio crackled. "One-oh-eight, Tampa."

"This is one-oh-eight, go ahead."

"I have the results of that license check you wanted. The tag comes back to a 1979 two-door Ford, model Thunderbird, registered to a Robert T. Grantham, address 734 Southwest Avenue B, Winter Haven, Polk County, Florida. Do you want a repeat on that?''

''I have it, thanks. One-oh-eight clear.''

The patrol sergeant stifled a yawn. Waiting was not something he enjoyed. ''I think I'm going to go start seeing what we can learn about this Grantham.'' He looked toward the back of the benign-seeming blue and white Thunderbird. ''I wonder if . . .'' He shook his head. There was no way to know if that was Robert T. Grantham's blood in there—yet. ''If you need me for anything, squawk.''

''I will, thanks.''

Raley got out of the patrol car, taking with him his notepad in which, by long established habit, he wrote down the particulars of the radioed report on the Thunderbird's license plate. At the top of the day's notebook page was the date: May 19, 1987.

This particular Tuesday was turning out to be a busy one for the Tampa International Airport Police.

Sgt. Raley wondered what kind of a day it was—or had been—for Robert T. Grantham.

3

''So what do you think, officer? Do we have a body here or don't we?''

Houck suppressed a shudder, but he didn't look away. There was an eerie fascination to the disclosure that he did not want to see—in one way—but that he felt impelled to witness in another.

FDLE crime lab analyst Ed Guenther winked at Houck, then bore down on the handle of the poor man's pry bar (a long, heavy screwdriver) and with a swift yank popped the trunk lock on the dusty Thunderbird that he'd already photographed.

For Houck's benefit Guenther waited several long moments before slowly, and with a maximum amount of drama, disclosing the contents of the trunk.

The trunk was empty, at least as far as bodies were concerned. Guenther had already known that it would be, and for the same reason Manny Pondakos did: there was a lack of smell. A body left unrefrigerated in the heat and humidity of the Florida climate will quickly deteriorate, and in the process announce itself in a most unmistakable manner. If exposed to the heat of the sun and to moisture, in fact, it can become impossible for the casual observer to distinguish between male and female corpses within days. Guenther was well aware of this thanks to his experience at the scenes of numerous natural deaths—and otherwise—all too often otherwise. Guenther grinned at Houck and then laughed. For an FDLE analyst, this was an exceedingly simple day at the office.

After completing his on-site photos, Guenther arranged for Robert Grantham's Thunderbird to be towed to the laboratory for the exhaustively detailed processing that is necessary if court-admissible evidence is to be obtained.

As part of that very exacting process Ed Guenther followed close behind the tow truck—just in case something dropped off the Thunderbird in transit.

At this stage of the investigation—before it was even known for certain if a crime had indeed been committed—there was no such thing as inconsequential evidence, and nothing would be allowed to become lost

Jetween Tampa International and the FDLE laboratory.

While the FDLE was busy with that phase of this current investigation, James Houck remained busy in parking area B2.

First, he took down descriptions and license numbers on the cars surrounding the blood-soaked Ford—in case the owners of those cars needed to be contacted to determine if anyone had noticed anything that might prove helpful—then Houck returned to the TIA police station situated within the huge terminal building.

Grateful for the air-conditioning after the oppressive heat of the parking garage, Houck took little time to cool off before getting down to business. A glance at his watch indicated that it was already past the hour for his usual lunch break. But today that would just have to be postponed for a while longer. Right now, there were more important things that had to be done.

Houck called parking lot manager Jim Slayton and asked when the blue and white Thunderbird entered the lot.

While it might normally be thought farfetched to ask someone when one particular car among literally thousands first appeared inside the jurisdictional limits of the airport police, the question was a much more reasonable one than most parking garage patrons might realize.

There is, in fact, a highly detailed daily log of the vehicles left in each section of the parking lot, with every license number being recorded via a handheld data collection module, which, at the end of each work shift, is downloaded into a computer master record. The computer is programmed to flag any vehicle that has been in place forty-five days or longer. If a car or truck exceeds that limit, the authorities then try to determine if the owner is indeed on an extended trip or if the airport has been used—as frequently happens—as the dumping ground for an unwanted or possibly stolen vehicle.

And as easy as it is to determine approximately when a car enters the airport lot, it is even simpler to find out when a car has left a lot.

In addition to the daily inventory record, the license plate number of every automobile is notated on the time ticket turned in when a car leaves and the amount due is calculated. There is a convex security mirror mounted at each ticket booth, which allows booth attendants to see and record the tag number of each car that comes through.

The reason airport parking lot operators go to this trouble is in order to foil patrons who may wish to avoid paying long-term parking fees by securing, either by theft or new issue, parking tickets claiming their car has been in the lot for only a brief period. By comparing the license number of departing cars with the daily inventory records, the lot attendants can quickly verify the amount of time a given vehicle has been on the airport grounds.

There are, however, other uses for the information, of which Houck's call now served as an example.

"What was that number again?" Slayton asked.

Houck repeated it for him.

"Hold the line while I pull it up for you. This won't take a minute."

While Houck was waiting, Sgt. Raley came into the room.

"Did you find anything on the owner?" Houck asked him.

"We got a hit," Raley affirmed. "The Winter Haven Police Department has a bulletin out on him. I called them and got one of their detectives. And guess what?"

Houck lifted an eyebrow.

"The guy's ex-wife put a missing persons report out on him. Seems like he went to Las Vegas and was due to fly back by way of Orlando on May 7, but he never made it home. The ex called Orlando, and they told her the car—the same car, mind you—checked out of there on schedule on the seventh. No one knows what happened to him after that.''

''Maybe nobody knows, but judging by the inside of that Thunderbird, I think we can make an awful good guess,'' Houck offered.

Raley shrugged and would have said something, but Houck held a finger up to stop him for the moment. Slayton had come back on the line.

''I have your Ford, license 976HFB.''

''Great. What's the word on it?''

''It first appears on the inventory during the first watch on May 8. That puts it into the lot either late May 7 or in the very early morning hours on the eighth.''

''You're terrific. Thanks.''

''Any time.''

Houck disconnected and leaned back in his chair. ''You say this guy flew from Vegas to Orlando on May 7 and left their parking lot on that date?''

''That's what Winter Haven PD tells me.''

''May 7 is when the car first showed up here.''

''That means . . .''

''Yeah. That means the damn thing has been sitting in our lot, blood and all, for almost two weeks now.''

Raley shook his head. ''Two weeks. Jeez. What can you learn after all that much time?''

4

Ed Guenther pulled alongside the tow truck as it arrived at the FDLE Regional Crime Laboratory. He got out of his car and pushed the numbered combination on the electronic lock to the gate of the vehicle compound, causing it to swing open.

The driver of the tow truck backed the Thunderbird into a covered warehouse and then unhooked the vehicle. Guenther returned to his car and, after driving into the fenced-in area, closed the gates behind the departing tow truck.

After turning on the banks of powerful overhead lights and closing the large doors to the warehouse area, Guenther took his time assembling the tools of his meticulous trade, which included donning sterile surgical gloves and, most importantly, insuring that he had a large supply of plastic bags and evidence tape on hand.

Careful to avoid touching any interior surface lest he smudge a fingerprint or otherwise disturb potential evidence, Guenther's first task was to collect, catalog, and preserve every object that was not a part of the automobile itself.

Starting with the obvious, he first picked up, bagged,

then tagged each of the objects resting on the Thunderbird's untidy dashboard.

Among those were a pair of safety glasses, a Red Man chewing tobacco pouch, two ballpoint pens, a can of Fresh Scent air freshener, and one unsmoked Doral cigarette.

In addition to bagging each item, sealing the bags with evidence tape and tagging each bag with an evidence number, Guenther also notated the items by number on a legal pad and noted where each article had been found in the car.

It was tedious, time-consuming work, but the information so meticulously obtained could become vital to an investigation and/or to legal proceedings afterward. Ed Guenther knew the importance of his work and made no attempt to hurry it.

On the front passenger seat, laid out in what seemed a hasty attempt to cover the bloodstains from view, was a section of the *Lakeland Ledger* newspaper dated May 2, 1987. There was also an empty Red Man chewing tobacco box.

Finished with the preliminary collection of items from the dashboard and front seat, Guenther shifted his attention to the litter on the passenger side floor.

There were a Marriott Host drinking cup, a scorecard from the Bartow Florida Golf Course, a GTE telephone bill, warranty information concerning 1979 Ford Thunderbird automobiles, three paper napkins, two Red Man chewing tobacco pouches, two empty 16-ounce Pepsi Cola bottles, an empty Budweiser beer bottle, an empty Riunite wine bottle, an empty 12-ounce Coca Cola can, a First Union Bank transaction receipt, a brown paper bag, a towel and, finally, an orange baseball cap.

Guenther took special care in handling the towel and baseball cap. Both of those appeared to have blood on them. And since the blood on the passenger seat upholstery was so obviously smeared, Guenther assumed that these were the items that had been used to wipe down the seat.

His search thus far limited to the obvious, Guenther now pulled out a flashlight and began examining the floor far forward underneath the dashboard.

He grunted with satisfaction as the light reflected brightly on a small, silvery object there—first, the one item and then, close to it, another.

Guenther leaned into the car and felt a small thrill as he got a better look at what he had found here: cartridge casings—two of them. A pair of silver-colored casings in .22 rimfire caliber.

Careful to avoid touching the tiny casings, Guenther used the tip end of a ballpoint pen to lift each one and drop it into a separate evidence bag.

Feeling quite thoroughly rewarded now and his interest quickened, Guenther pushed the passenger seat forward and began cataloging the trash in the backseat and floorboard area.

The obvious items were not of immediate interest, but they, too, had to be collected and recorded with thoroughgoing care. Out of the backseat area came a white hardhat, a First Union Bank money envelope, an air flight packet from TranStar Airlines, an empty Doral cigarette carton, and a wooden walking cane. Also on the floor were two plastic bags and a check drawn on the account of Bob's Insulated Roofing. And then. . . .

Another slim .22 cartridge casing lay on the car floor immediately behind the blood-smeared passenger seat.

And finally one more item came to light, jammed into the gap between the upholstered seat cushion and the back of the seat itself: a fourth and final empty .22 cartridge.

Four cartridge casings—and an incredible amount of blood.

It required no exceptional powers of deduction to reach a conclusion that there just really might be a connection there.

5

Business as usual. But then for some people business sometimes involves blood. Ed Williams, chief of the Florida Department of Law Enforcement's Tampa bureau, is one of those people. He hung up the telephone, accepting the news he had just been given without emotion. This, after all, was the business he and his people are in.

The FDLE is made up of several divisions, among them a Division of Criminal Investigations. The DCI offers assistance to local police departments and sheriff's offices. It also has the authority to conduct investigations on its own, particularly when the jurisdictional responsibilities of other agencies are unclear or indeed unknown.

The bureau chief of the Tampa office (an office which until recently was located not in Tampa, by the way, but in neighboring and much smaller Temple Terrace) left his own desk and entered the squad bay. At the moment the only investigator on the premises was Special Agent Ray Velboom.

Williams was not at all unhappy with Velboom as the logical choice to receive this new assignment. One of forty-five agents working under Williams's supervision,

Ray Velboom was known to his colleagues as a good man and a dogged investigator.

Velboom—age thirty-seven and divorced—was thought of by male friends as a rugged guy, with a neatly trimmed beard giving him something of the appearance of a mountain man. Women tended to view him as a handsome and cuddly teddy bear sort.

Williams, however, was not interested in his investigator's appearance but in the man's abilities.

"Have you heard about the car Manny Pondakos found at the airport?" Williams asked.

"Sure. That was, what, a couple days ago, right?"

Williams nodded. "Two days."

"He turned it over to the airport police, is that right?"

"Yes, and they turned it right back around to us."

"What is it—a car or a boomerang?"

"The deal is this, Ray. TIA claims it shouldn't be their case because the physical evidence indicates the crime—if there was a crime—couldn't have been committed at the airport. Their reasoning is sound, actually. If a crime took place—and that has yet to be proven either way—there should have been blood spilled outside the car as well as in it. Moving a body covered with that much blood would be almost impossible without smearing it around, dripping on the ground, like that. So, they have a good argument that whatever happened took place outside their jurisdiction, and they were just lucky enough to have the car dumped on them there." Williams shrugged. "Besides, they don't have either the manpower or the expertise to run a major crime investigation. They'd likely want to bring us in even if the jurisdiction clearly did belong to them."

"All right, I can buy that."

"The next logical authority in line would be Winter Haven's PD. There's a missing persons report out on the owner of the car, and Winter Haven is where he lives."

"Or lived," Velboom interjected.

"Anyway, Winter Haven says since there's no body and no physical evidence in their jurisdiction, they don't want it."

Velboom grinned. "So it's right back in Manny's lap, huh?" There was more than a hint of irony there in that it was Manny Pondakos who found the case to begin with, and then passed the ball to TIA. Now the thing bounced right back to its originator.

Bureau Chief Ed Williams tugged at his collar and stretched his neck. And Ray Velboom sat up straighter in his chair, his attention becoming suddenly focused. Williams's mannerism was a sure signal that he had something important on his mind. The bureau chief might not realize that, but his agents certainly all recognized it.

Velboom guessed—hoped—what might be coming next. As a special agent supervisor, Manny Pondakos oversaw the work of other agents but did not carry a caseload of his own. So the responsibility would be placed on some member of the Tampa staff. Ray Velboom quite frankly hoped he would get it. This one looked to have the makings of a case a man could sink his teeth into.

Ed Williams let go of his shirt collar and said, "Ray, I'm going to give this case to you. I want you to concentrate solely on this for the time being. Contact Sgt. Dan Raley at TIA and tell him you will be the agent in charge from this point on. He can fill you in on everything they have. From that point on, Ray, the case is yours."

Velboom's response was a very large grin.

6

Ray Velboom's first stop was at the Tampa International Airport police station where Sgt. Raley quickly filled him in on what the TIA police knew and gave him a hand-drawn diagram of the car and surroundings in the terminal parking lot.

From there the FDLE investigator made the short trip to the crime lab, which is housed separately from the other offices. Once there, he was directed to the impounded Thunderbird, which was being kept in a carefully controlled environment.

"Looks like blood to me," Velboom said, referring to the dark stains that covered so much of the upholstery material in the dusty automobile.

"As a matter of fact, it is blood," lab analyst Scott Carey affirmed. "We took samples and tested them. It's human blood, all right. Type A."

Velboom made a note of the information. One of the things he would have to do as soon as possible was to find out the blood type of Robert Grantham, the owner of the impounded Ford. "I'd like to see the evidence you collected too, of course."

"This way." Carey took the investigator to the evidence vault, which is *very* carefully controlled because even a hint of suspicion about the security of evidence, such as the mere possibility that an unauthorized party might have had access to the materials, would make the most crucial evidence inadmissible in a court of law, and he brought out the items which lab tech Ed Guenther had so very meticulously gathered and recorded days earlier.

Velboom first went over the written list, then examined the bagged and tagged collection.

The .22 cartridge casings brought an approving whistle to his lips. No one had mentioned those to him before, and he inspected them closely. All four were the same make: CCI, manufacturer of a popular extremely high-velocity .22 cartridge. Ballistics testing would easily determine if the cartridges were all fired by the same weapon. Examination under high magnification would show if a single firing pin and/or extractor left markings on the relatively soft metal of the casings.

Velboom added a copy of the evidence list to the growing collection of paperwork he was building on this new case, then prepared to leave. But the lab analyst stopped him—he was smiling.

"What is it you've been holding back?"

"The best for the last, you know," Carey confessed. "We didn't just type the blood in the car."

"No?"

"Leroy Parker, the crime-scene expert from the Orlando office, stopped by the other day. We asked him to take a look at your T-Bird."

"Yeah?" Velboom's interest quickened. Parker (no relation to the famous outlaw Butch Cassidy whose real name was also Leroy Parker) had an excellent reputation among those who chased modern day outlaws with modern day methods.

"Parker took a look at the blood splatter patterns inside the car. His opinion is that the blood spray is consistent with gunshots to the head of a seated victim."

Velboom was mildly disappointed. After all, you can't hardly stand up in the front seat of a '79 T-Bird.

Carey, however, was not finished.

"Well, after Parker was through, and after the things he was telling us, we asked the medical examiner to come by, too."

"Yeah?"

"Darn right. He went over the quantity of blood that was found in the car. You know, all those stains on the seats and carpet and more soaked into the towel and cap and blotted-up by those newspapers. You know what his opinion is?"

Velboom shook his head.

"According to the ME, one human person could not lose that much blood and survive. No chance. Velboom, it looks like you've got a murder on your hands."

7

Ray Velboom returned to his office to find a message waiting for him requesting him to call FDLE special agent Steve Davenport in the agency's Lakeland office.

For administrative purposes, the Florida Department of Law Enforcement divides the state into four districts. Tampa serves as headquarters for the Central Regional Office Bureau, where Ed Williams is in charge of all the investigative staff throughout the region, including the Lakeland bureau where Steve Davenport was assigned.

Velboom was already familiar with Davenport. The man's reputation was that of an excellent investigator. A nice-looking man with dark brown hair worn slightly long, Davenport's hazel eyes could harden into a stare that would intimidate even the most stubborn witness, or could become soft and sympathetic to charm a witness into revealing what the agent wanted to know.

Like Velboom, Davenport was unmarried. Which, although neither man could know it at the time, would prove to be a blessing. Both Ray Velboom and Steve Davenport would soon be devoting nearly all their waking moments to the case that was just now falling into their laps.

"Velboom here. You wanted a call back?"

"Yeah, Ray, thanks for getting back to me so soon. Are you familiar with the name Robin Boney?"

Velboom gave the question the courtesy of reflection, but his answer did not change after he had time to think about it. "No, it rings no bells. Should it?"

"Not necessarily, but she's the niece of a guy from Winter Haven named Robert Grantham. The duty officer told me you've been assigned as case agent on something involving him. Is that right?"

"Sure is." Velboom filled Davenport in on what they knew about Robert Grantham. Or, more accurately, brought the Lakeland man up to date on what they unfortunately did not know but suspected. "What's the deal with Boney, Steve?"

"She called here a little while ago. It seems she saw something in the newspaper about her uncle's car being found abandoned at Tampa International. I asked her why she called us instead of going direct to you. She said Tampa is a long distance call for her—she lives in Winter Haven—and Lakeland is local. So she tried us first. I told her I'd check with you guys and get back to her."

"Did she say anything about Grantham?"

"No, and since I didn't know anything about the case,

I didn't ask. Do you think the guy is dead?''

"Somebody seems to be, but we don't know who. You wouldn't believe the amount of blood.''

"Any leads?'' Davenport asked.

"This Robin Boney of yours could be the first.''

"Could it have been an accident?''

"I don't see any way,'' Velboom said. "One person losing that much blood would be dead. And any combination of people bleeding that bad would've gone to a hospital, not the airport. Another thing: we found four spent cartridge casings in the car.''

"Those could have been there for months.''

"Sure, and the Easter Bunny could show up at Thanksgiving this year. My personal opinion is that Robert Grantham got whacked.''

"Look, Winter Haven is right down the road from our shop. If you need any help over here . . .''

"As a matter of fact, I could use a favor. Call your friend Boney back and set up a time when we can meet with her. Also with the wife—ex-wife, I mean—I've got her name written down someplace. . . .'' A few moments later he came back on the line. "Jacquelyn O'Hara, that's it. She's the one who filed the missing persons report with the Winter Haven PD.''

"I'll see what I can do. You're free to come running?''

"Any time. Just name it.''

They disconnected, and while Steve Davenport was looking for Jacquelyn O'Hara's telephone number, he received another call from Robin Boney. She wanted to know if he had learned anything yet about her uncle.

Five minutes later he was back on the phone to Velboom. "I told her I couldn't give her any information on the telephone, Ray, and she suggested that I come see her tomorrow afternoon. Better yet, when I asked where she would like to meet us, guess what?''

"Am I going to like this?''

"I think so. She wants us to meet her at Jacquelyn O'Hara's place."

"You're kidding."

"Would I do that to you?"

"Yeah, but I hope you aren't this time."

"It's true. She was real helpful. Explained to me who this O'Hara was and everything. I didn't let on we already knew about the lady and wanted to speak with her, too."

"Sounds perfect, Steve. I'll drive over there right after lunch, and we'll go together to talk with Boney and O'Hara. The next logical step with this thing, I think, will be to find out just who this missing and maybe dead Robert Grantham is. Or was."

8

On Saturday, January 10, 1987, four months before it was found abandoned in parking area B2 at Tampa International Airport, the white-top blue 1979 Ford Thunderbird was baking in the mid-morning sunshine at a used car dealership.

Dave's Used Cars used to be a gasoline station. In its current incarnation the business was a halfway house for aging automobiles not quite yet ready for wreckage. The normal run of offerings on the lot was such that the eight-year-old Ford, which at least had all its paint intact, stood out like a sapphire tossed in among a handful of

Cracker Jack prizes. Its gleaming chrome and snappy wax job fell under the eyes of thousands of potential buyers each day on busy US 17-92 in tiny Eagle Lake, Florida, just south of Winter Haven.

The offer drew a nibble when a pickup truck bearing a sign for Bob's Insulated Roofing pulled into the lot, and a large man with graying hair emerged. The man leaned heavily on a dark brown wooden cane as he nodded to the salesman who had stepped outside. The man with the cane limped slowly toward the Thunderbird.

"That's a fine car you're looking at there," said a salesman. "Full-size and all the power in the world, but driving it is like riding on a cloud. You know what I mean? Smooth and slick and easy to drive. Plenty of comfort, too. It's loaded, has everything you could ever want. All the goodies, and it's practically like new—in and out. This one really is as clean as everybody claims their cars are. You won't find another one this nice, not anyplace."

Robert Grantham leaned down to peer through the windows at the white leather upholstery. He tried the handle, but the car was locked.

"Let me get you a key," the salesman offered, hurrying back to his office before the prospect had time to respond.

Grantham edged slowly around the car. It really did look as clean as the salesman claimed.

The man returned and unlocked the driver's side door, holding it open for Grantham, who laid his cane on the backseat floorboard and slid heavily behind the wheel.

"The seat controls are—"

"I see them."

"If you want to take it for a drive I can put a tag on and—"

"No, I don't have time for that. I'm on my way to a golf date."

The salesman gave Grantham, and his cane, a look of

muted skepticism, but of course he said nothing. Golf date? Oh, well. You have to put up with a lot of lookers if you expect to winnow that one lone buyer out of the bunch.

"How much?" Grantham asked, shaking the steering wheel like a small boy pretending to drive his daddy's car.

"Thirty-nine fifty. Were you, uh, wanting to trade the pickup?"

"No. No trade. I might want to finance it, though. Your sign says 'Buy Here, Pay Here.' Is that right?"

"If there's no trade-in involved, I might be able to work with you on that price some. If you can come up with a reasonable amount down, that is."

Grantham said nothing. But he ran his hand over the leather on the back of the passenger seat and craned his neck around to look into the backseat area. The back of the car looked like it had never seen any use more serious than the transportation of a bag of groceries now and then. There was a small, hardly noticeable sun-crack on the left side of the dashboard panel. But that seemed to be the worst blemish visible. The car was definitely cherry.

"Look, I don't want to miss my tee time. Do you have a card?"

"Yeah, sure." The salesman was willing to think maybe this guy really did have a golf date. He came up with the requested card, which the prospect tucked into his shirt pocket. "If there's anything I can do—"

"I'll let you know." Grantham got out of the car, retrieved his cane, and headed back toward his truck. He had to drive all the way down to Wauchula to meet his golfing partners. All in all the trip would have been much more pleasant in the quiet, full-sized luxury of a T-Bird.

He'd always had a weakness for Thunderbirds. Along with many other weaknesses, it was true. But this car
. . . he really liked this car. A car like that said something

about a man. Said the sort of things women like. Or so Robert Grantham believed.

Still, they were asking almost four thousand. They'd come down off that price. But how far, he wondered.

Not that he was going to buy the car, of course. He didn't actually need it. He only wanted it.

But damn, it was clean. A man doesn't find a T-Bird that clean and nice just any old day of the week.

Scowling a little, Grantham gunned the engine of his pickup and rolled south on the highway, anxious now to meet his friends in Wauchula lest they miss their tee time.

9

Bob Grantham propped up his bum right leg and reached down to rub it. The massaging didn't make him feel any better—the leg always ached the day after a round on a golf course—but he made the effort anyway.

Damn leg—it was a nuisance—much worse than a mere nuisance really—that just wouldn't go away. It had been the better part of a year, since the previous May, when he had slipped. One small, incautious misstep, that was all it had been. The problem was that at the time he'd been ambling along on the steep-pitched roof of a two-story home. Tending to business, that was what he'd been doing. It was a perfectly normal, everyday job of reshingling. Until he made that one small slip.

He'd fallen (though he had no recollection of it at all, but he certainly knew it happened) forty feet, striking the ground feet first and dropping in a shattered heap, where later the ambulance crew found him after the owner of the house he was working on called 911 for help.

He was lucky. That's what the doctors said. He could have broken his back. He could have hit his head and been killed. He was lucky. They kept telling him that. Except they didn't feel his pain when they were saying that to him over and over again. Damned if he felt lucky.

Both legs were broken and both ankles. The right was the worst off. After waiting out a cardiac false alarm that delayed the reconstructive surgery for several days, and always afterward he could not help but wonder if things might have come out better if they hadn't had to wait like that, the surgeons rebuilt his right ankle with enough metal to stock a small hardware store. Six days later they operated again to repair the left ankle, but that one needed only a single pin.

Ever since then he needed the use of either a cane for very short distances or a wheelchair in order to get around.

There were no guarantees the legs would ever get better, either. That rankled him. But then once a man gets past the age of fifty, even if only barely past it like he was at 51, the healing process is not so quick and simple as it used to be.

His morose reverie was interrupted by the sound of someone knocking on his front door. A moment later he could hear the door being opened, and a woman's voice called, ''Bob?''

''In here.'' He reached for the remote control to turn the sound down on the television.

He hadn't recognized the voice, but it was the new girl Karen who came in. Karen . . . H something. Hass . . . Hos . . . he couldn't remember her last name and didn't want to bother going back to the spare room he used as an office to look it up.

Bob Grantham employed a good many women in his roofing crews. Not that they were particularly good roofers. His opinion was that men made much better roofers and much better employees too. But there were compensations. Oh yes, there were.

Karen came into the family room and dropped into a limp, sweaty lump on the sofa. "I came to check the work schedule for this week."

Grantham nodded and gave her a looking over, not bothering to try to hide the direction his gaze was roving. This girl Karen—she was no beauty—but the only reason he would kick her out of bed would be because there was more thrashing room on the floor.

She was wearing shorts and a halter, and her dishwater blond hair was pulled back under a damp terrycloth headband. Her thighs were meaty and plump enough, but she didn't have much upstairs. About a good B-cup, Grantham judged, or a scant C. He liked big breasts on a woman. But he wasn't a complainer. No sir—no one could say that about Robert Theist Grantham. He appreciated whatever was put in front of him. "The list is right here. You can look at it if you want."

He didn't offer to hand it to her, only pointing to a pile of papers on the small table beside his chair; so, after a moment, Karen got up and came over to lean across her employer and reach for the work sheet.

Casually, as if it were quite an automatic and normal thing to do, Bob Grantham laid the flat of his hand on the warm, damp flesh between Karen's halter and the top of her shorts. When she straightened upright, his hand just as automatically and naturally slid lower so that it cupped one cheek of her backside.

Karen pulled back half a step, just out of his reach, while she looked over the schedule for the coming work week. "I was hoping for more hours than this, Bob. You promised me I'd have at least thirty-five, thirty-six hours and this is, what, twenty something?''

''Everybody wants more hours. You know that.''

''Not everybody has three kids at home. You know?''

''Let me see the list. Hold it down here. No, closer.'' He blinked and rubbed at his eyes as if they were giving him trouble. ''A little closer. That's better. Let me see what I have you down for.''

His hand curled around behind her leg and slid in between her thighs. Then higher. The woman's body stiffened.

''If you need the hours, Karen, maybe we can work something out.'' He smiled. ''You know?'' And the fingers of his right hand found the hem of her shorts and went on an exploratory excursion inside. Bob Grantham discovered that she wasn't wearing panties. And she really did want more hours on the work schedule for the coming week. Oh yes, she did.

10

''You're a son of a bitch, Bob. You know that, don't you?''

He gave her a smile that combined amusement with affection. ''What is it this time, Jackie?''

''You. Everything. Buying another car. Jesus, Bob, if there's anything you don't need, it's another car. Or another bill.''

"Aw, I'm good for it. You know that."

"You just don't care, do you? You never think ahead. Do you know what's wrong with you, Bob?"

"Sure. Lots of things. As you keep telling me. Now keep your eyes on the road, Jackie, and watch for the car lot."

They were in Jacquelyn O'Hara's car nearing the town of Eagle Lake. Grantham had called ahead. The Thunderbird was still there, and he wanted it.

Life was lousy enough without a man having to deny himself every small pleasure. His ex-wife might not understand that, but he did.

And what the hell. As ex-wives go, Jackie wasn't so bad. They had been divorced for nearly two years, but they still saw each other fairly often, still called on each other for advice or help or whatever, as now, when Bob needed a lift to the car place so he would be free to drive the T-Bird home.

Sometimes he thought they got along better now than they had when they were married.

He pulled a pouch of Red Man out and stuffed a wad of the dark, rich tobacco into his cheek, ignoring the look Jackie gave him.

"Robert!" Her voice was a low growl.

"Aw, I'm housebroke. I won't spit on your floor." She might have said more, but he straightened in his seat and pointed. "That's it up there. Slow down. Looks good, doesn't she?"

"The blue one?"

"Yeah. Gorgeous, isn't it?"

"It looks very nice, Bob." She pulled into Dave's Used Cars, the wheels of her vehicle bumping loudly, and came to a stop. "I'll wait here to make sure everything goes all right."

"You don't have to do that. I don't need anybody hanging around like my mother walking me to kiddy-garten, dammit, and waiting on the curb for me to come out. Go on. I don't need you.''

Jacquelyn O'Hara gave him another look, this one as much resignation as it was exasperation. There was no point in venturing a comment. She knew that. ''Enjoy your car, Bob.''

''I'll take you for a spin later on, okay? We can go out and get some barbecue or something. Just the two of us.''

''Sure, Bob. Whatever.''

Grantham got his cane out of the backseat of his ex-wife's car and limped into the used car dealer's office.

All he could think about at the moment was that absolutely fine blue and white Ford Thunderbird out there. It was going to be his. Bob Grantham liked acquiring things. And if he liked something, well, it didn't really matter what that thing cost. The important question was could he have it, not could he afford it.

11

The T-Bird was everything he'd hoped it would be. Smooth, quiet, a ride so soft it felt like it was gliding along above the road instead of riding on top of it. And powerful? If he could just figure out a way to make the tires fit onto the tracks, he was sure the Thunderbird could do double duty as a railroad locomotive.

It was much too nice a day to go back to work. Besides, by now all the roofing crews should be out on jobs. There wouldn't be anything happening back at the house that Jackie couldn't handle. She would answer the phone if it rang and take down any messages. Why spoil such a fine day now?

Instead of going back home he turned the polished nose of the blue T-Bird south, cut over through Bartow and took State Road 60 west through Mulberry and Brandon to Tampa where he paused briefly to admire the ships tied up at the downtown docks; he continued north again to Interstate 275, then drove west, not because he particularly wanted to go to St. Petersburg, but simply because he enjoyed the view from the long Howard Frankland Bridge where it crossed Old Tampa Bay. The view from the Howard Frankland was the sort of thing they put on postcards. And with good reason: it was spectacular.

The powerful Thunderbird carried him in comfort on across the Pinellas County peninsula to the gulf beaches, where he trolled slowly in search of local color—colorful bikinis, that is.

Unfortunately, it was the wrong time of year for beach cruising. The nubile young things who favored t-backs and string bikinis were still in school, and the beach goers who showed up on a weekday in winter tended to be in their sixties or older and, depending on their outdoor habits, looked either like dark tanned leather or lumpy boiled suet. Neither extreme was at all appealing, nor were the dowdy swimsuits these geriatric jennies wore.

Disappointed, he stopped at a gulf front tavern for a short one—or two—then went back out to the Thunderbird.

The car fired up with a muted, mellow rumble, and just for the fun of it he jabbed the accelerator hard as he pulled out of the lot. The tires spun on the hard-packed shell, then bit with a squeal as they hit asphalt.

Bob Grantham laughed aloud and lifted off the accelerator before some cop came along and spoiled things.

He found a bridge back to the mainland and followed that road—back to the interstate.

The cruise control worked like a charm, and the radio had a good sound to it.

It was late afternoon by now, and he thought about calling Jackie at the office. They'd said something about going for a ride this evening. Barbecue, right?

There was no hurry, though. Jackie could wait.

Since he was already this far, and practically had to pass right by it, there was no reason why he shouldn't stop in at the Club 92. After all, Seffner is between Tampa and Winter Haven, isn't it? Never mind that he'd have to get off the Interstate and swing down to US 92; that was no problem. The T-Bird didn't mind another mile or two, so why not?

Grinning, Bob Grantham nudged the accelerator pedal with his toe, allowing the speedometer needle to creep up another five, ten, twelve miles per hour.

Yeah, this was a *really* good day.

12

Club 92 was one of Bob Grantham's favorite haunts, not only because he liked the band that played there, but more importantly because of his occasional successes in picking up women there.

A plain, cream-colored building, the bar sported the declaration ''Drive Thru Package'' painted in bold lettering on the front wall. A large, billboard-type sign bore the name of the place plus the enticement ''Cut Rate Liquors,'' as if the obvious were not quite obvious enough. On this particular evening the marquee attached to the sign advertised entertainment by the Abbott Brothers Band.

Bob Grantham parked his new Thunderbird in the lot behind Club 92 and spit out the wad of Red Man he'd been working on.

He paused inside the door to let his eyes adjust to the dim interior of the club. Noted more for its action than its atmosphere, Club 92 was usually dark, loud, and busy. This evening, however, because it was still early on a weekday, the bandstand and tiny dance floor to his left were empty. At the bar to his right he could see only one solitary drinker. That was enough to make Grantham smile, though. The lone other customer was female. He blinked, trying to hurry the process of adjusting his vision to the light level, and began his halting progress toward the lady who had an old-fashioned in front of her.

Young, sleek, and lovely—that was what Bob Grantham craved.

This one was . . . a lot of years from being young or sleek or lovely.

Plump and in her forties at the earliest—and perhaps fiftysomething if you scraped some of the makeup away—she had hair in that bright, brassy shade of auburn that comes from kitchen-sink dye jobs. Her hair was teased high and swept upward in a bubble that surrounded her head. She wore intensely dark mascara and false eyelashes capable of resisting a stiff breeze.

Grantham did not mind any of that. His attention was focused on the way she was dressed—for action—definitely for action. She was wearing a too-small leather skirt, an even smaller knit shirt, and no brassiere.

She didn't appear to take notice when the newcomer with the cane took the stool next to hers. But then she very likely was used to being approached by strangers.

"Evening, Bob. What will it be tonight?" The bartender placed a napkin in front of him.

"A Bud for me, and give this young lady another of whatever she's drinking."

If he had expected a reaction—and indeed he did— he was disappointed. The woman acted like she hadn't heard.

"Hi, hon, how are you?"

She didn't so much as look at him.

The bartender returned with a bourbon on the rocks for the woman and a bottled beer and glass for Grantham. The man filled the glass and set the nearly empty bottle down.

"How much is that?" Grantham asked even though he knew good and well what the charge would be.

The barman announced the total, and Grantham pulled a thick wallet out of his back pocket, holding it practically underneath his would-be companion's nose as he thumbed through the wad of bills he routinely carried there. He favored twenties for the most part, with a few fives and tens thrown in as well. No fifties or hundreds, though. They didn't have enough bulk for his liking.

He riffled through the wallet twice, sure he had the woman's attention by now, and selected a ten-dollar bill. "Keep the change," he said rather grandly.

The bartender left. The woman gave Bob Grantham a look for the first time. "Thanks for the drink, mister."

"Mister, that's what they used to call my daddy. I'm Bob."

"So, thanks for the drink, Bob."

"You're welcome, miss, uh, miss . . ." He grinned at her and winked.

"Ivy," she said. "Ivy Brown." Ivy maybe—he conceded—Brown, unlikely. Not that he cared.

"Now, I'm just real glad to meet you, Ivy Brown. It's a real treat for me to see such a pretty woman in here. That makes it a real good evening for me. And do you know what, Ivy Brown? I think this is going to be a real good evening for you, too."

"Yeah, how's that, Bob?"

"Well, I got this problem, see, and I think you can help me with it."

She pulled back a little. "Problem, Bob?"

"That's right, Ivy. You see, I've got just too damn much money in my wallet here. I was hoping maybe you could take a hundred or so off me and kind of help me out."

"I always try and help a person whenever I can, Bob. That's just the way I am." There was a hint of a smile tickling the corners of her heavily made-up mouth now.

"I was hoping you'd have that attitude, Ivy. I really was." He winked at her again and once more pulled out his wallet. He reached in with thumb and forefinger and pulled out a thick sheaf of bills that he did not bother to count. He dropped them onto the bar surface and reached for his cane. "Excuse me for a minute, Ivy. I got to go to the can."

"I'll be here when you get back, Bob," she promised.

And so she was. The money, however, had disappeared.

"I'm ready anytime you are, sweetie," Ivy said as her "date" for the evening returned.

A few other customers were coming into the bar by now and the Abbott Brothers Band was setting up on the small stage beyond the dance floor.

Bob waved to one of the band members, Jimmy Abbott, who used to be married to Grantham's niece, Robin Boney. He gave a wink and a leer to another of the band members, Debbie Ware, but Debbie ignored him.

Moving at his slow, deliberate pace, Bob Grantham

followed Ivy Brown outside and took her around to the handsome white-top blue Thunderbird.

Inside Club 92 Jimmy Abbott leaned over and made a joking reference to Grantham.

"Lying Bob? That son of a bitch," Debbie said, "he isn't funny. His chasing tail is going to catch up with him someday too." She scowled. "I hope."

Realizing that this was a subject not worth ruffling Debbie's feathers over, Jimmy Abbott put his concentration back on business, where it belonged.

13

Steve Davenport ran the palm of one hand over his hair, smoothing it back above his right ear. The gesture drew a chuckle, but no actual comment, from Ray Velboom. Before Steve might have had a chance to say something to Velboom, the door was opened in response to their ring.

"Yes?"

The FDLE special agents identified themselves. The young woman—a slightly plump blond in her mid-twenties—was Robin Boney. Behind her was the owner of the home, Mrs. Jacquelyn O'Hara, an attractive middle-aged woman with red hair. Davenport and Velboom offered to display their identification to the women, but the formality was declined. "Come in, please. You can sit over there. Have you found out anything about Bob yet? Do you know what's happened to him?''

Velboom smiled. "Usually this works better if we ask our questions first.''

"And if you don't mind, ladies,'' Davenport put in, "we would like to speak with each of you separately. Then perhaps later we can all talk. Would that be all right?''

Apart from the obvious benefit of not having one potential witness overhear the answers of another, a person being interviewed is always more candid if he or she does not have to edit responses to meet the expectations of someone else listening in.

The women agreed, and Robin Boney went into a back bedroom, closing the door behind her, leaving Jacquelyn O'Hara in the living room with the FDLE special agents.

Wanting to start with a simple, comfortable, nonthreatening discussion, Ray Velboom leaned back and asked, as if not yet quite ready to begin the interview, Jacquelyn how she and Grantham first met.

"That was in 1972,'' she recalled. "I'm an LPN— that's a licensed practical nurse—but at the time I was working in an unemployment office in Memphis, Tennessee. Bob came in looking for work.'' She laughed. "Actually, he seemed more interested in me than in finding a job. But I ignored his flirting and sent him off on an interview.''

"Did he get the job?''

"No. They were going to hire him, but then they ran a background check and found out about his criminal record.''

"He had a criminal past?''

"Oh, nothing really important. Just a lot of little things, none of them serious. You know.''

The agents in fact did not know; but they very soon would.

"He didn't get that job,'' Jacquelyn continued, "but

he kept coming into the office, trying to get me to go out with him. I finally agreed to go out on one date with him. I mean, I know it sounds funny now, after everything that's happened between us, but at the time I thought he was crude and loud and obnoxious. And I suppose he was all those things. But he could also be really sweet and caring, too. I mean, he could make a woman feel like she was the only really and truly important person in the whole world, at least as far as he was concerned. I liked that about him, and that's the truth.'' She shrugged. ''Anyway, we dated for a while, and I guess I kind of fell in love with the guy. When he asked me to marry him, I think I was more surprised than anybody that I said yes. We were married there in Memphis in July—the twenty-third it was—in July of 1972.''

''And when did you come to Florida?''

''Not long after we were married. Bob didn't care for Tennessee very much. He couldn't find any work there that he liked. And I think he felt ashamed because it was on his record up there about being in the mental health ward in a hospital for a while.'' Velboom and Davenport were busily using their pens. ''He wasn't in there very long, and it wasn't about anything serious. But he felt bad about it, and anyway, he missed Florida. He grew up around here, and this is where he likes it best. So I told him it was all right with me if he wanted to come back.''

The couple had moved to Winter Haven, where Bob Grantham was able to earn a good living in a series of jobs, mostly involving the citrus industry, which is the focus of the central Florida economy in and near Winter Haven.

Grantham's good fortune, however, was rarely shared with his Tennessee bride. When he had money in his pockets, he liked to use it to gamble—he loved to gamble and would wager on almost anything, including his frequent golf games, professional sports, college-level athletics, or very nearly anything else in which there was an element of chance—and to lavish it, along with his charm, on women.

To Bob Grantham, marriage was no barrier to a full, and widely broadcast, sex life.

"Is that why you divorced?"

"One of the reasons. The biggest one, I guess you could say. We got so we fought a lot, and I tried leaving him several different times. After a while . . ." She grimaced and shook her head.

After a moment, obviously unaware of the importance of what she was saying, she added, "I don't want you to think I didn't try. But all those women . . . and the times he'd just up and disappear . . ."

"Pardon me? You say he has been known to disappear before this?" Steve Davenport asked.

14

"Oh, I know what you're thinking, officer," Jacquelyn O'Hara said.

Neither he nor Ray Velboom was an "officer." They were special agents. This did not seem a good moment to get huffy over details, however.

"You're thinking Bob may just have up and disappeared again, aren't you? But I can tell you, this is different. His dogs, see. Bob would never go off and leave his dogs. Besides, leaving his car at the airport like that . . . that just isn't like him. No, this time it's real.''

''Still, we'd like you to tell us about those other times, if you don't mind.''

''They weren't anything . . . serious. If you know what I mean. He would just, like, take off sometimes. Just up and go away, to Las Vegas or New Orleans or wherever. He'd go off to gamble or he'd be chasing some sweet young thing . . . Bob just can't resist a nice-looking girl, especially if she's young and blond, you know? . . . and he'd take off and I wouldn't hear anything from him for a couple weeks, sometimes as long as several months.''

''And you wouldn't worry about him when he'd do that?''

''It's more like I'd get mad at him. Sure, I'd get mad at him when he'd go off like that. But it wasn't like there was anything to *worry* about. Except for once, maybe.'' She became quiet, as if in deep thought.

''Tell us about that one time that was different than the others,'' Ray Velboom prompted.

''That was . . . we weren't even living together at the time. We'd been fighting . . . the same old thing with his women and gambling and all . . . and this time I was really fed up. It was, let me see, 1979, I think. I went back up to Memphis and went back to nursing, like in private homes, taking care of old folks. I was doing real good, too. It felt kind of nice to be on my own again and not have to answer to him. We weren't divorced, see. Just not living together. We kept in touch, more or less, and while I was up in Memphis Bob wrote to say he was going to Louisiana. Well, I didn't much care. He was pretty much out of my life at the time. Then one night I'm fixing myself some supper and somebody knocks at my door. Who do you think it was but Bob. Just like that. He walks in and wants me to make him something to eat. So I did.

"He said he was working as a guard, some kind of guard job—I don't know the details—but it had to do with one of those offshore oil rigs and the tankers that came in with the oil from them. What he said, and I don't personally know if it's true or not, but what Bob said was that some of those ships carry more than oil. They bring drugs in from far off someplace and leave the drugs at the oil rigs because those are outside the country, sort of, and aren't, like, inspected or watched or anything. And then the helicopters that service the oil rigs bring these drugs in the rest of the way.

"What Bob had to do with all this, I wouldn't know. But he told me he'd come to warn me because since I was his wife I might be in trouble with some people he said were looking for him. And that's what he'd come for was to tell me that so I could watch myself.

"Of course there's one thing I have to tell you about Bob, if you don't already know it, and that is that the man wasn't always real careful with the truth. That's how he got his nickname with all his old buddies. Lyin' Bob Grantham. LBG, they called him sometimes. LBG— Lyin' Bob Grantham. They all knew him and thought it was kind of funny. But with him you just never knew.

"Anyway, getting back to what I was telling you about when he visited me that time. He spent the night . . . on my sofa, mind. We didn't sleep together. But I let him stay overnight. And then, the SOB, when I woke up that next morning he'd gone and taken my car. He took my nice '76 Thunderbird . . . it wasn't very old then, you see, and oh, it was nice . . . he filched my keys and took off with that nice red Thunderbird. We both have this thing about T-birds.

"A couple weeks later I got a call from the police at some place down in Louisiana. They found my Thunderbird along the side of the road, all smashed to pieces. There wasn't any sign of a driver or anything, and they checked the registration and called me about it. It was totaled, they said, and the insurance company told me there wasn't any point in me going down and trying to get the car because it was completely wrecked. So they sent me a check to cover the loss, and I never saw the car again after that.

"But I did see Bob again, of course." She sighed. "Sometimes I think I'd have been better off if I'd brought the car back and left him in a junkyard in Louisiana."

15

"The next time I saw Bob," Jacquelyn O'Hara told them, "was right after the police told me he was dead."

Ray Velboom's attention had been wandering. That little problem was cured now. And he could see the quickening interest in Steve Davenport's expression, too. "Who told you your ex-husband was dead, Mrs. O'Hara?"

"Oh, I didn't mean either of you, of course. I mean, that wasn't even this time . . . that is . . . I was still married to him, this time I'm talking about."

"But you said someone told you he was killed?"

"Yes. Sort of. This was, oh, quite a while after that time he took my car and wrecked it. Maybe it was part of the same trouble he said he was in then, or maybe it was something different, I don't really know."

Velboom and Davenport were both sitting on the

edges of their seats now, sitting forward a few inches off their seats like a pair of well-trained quail dogs on point. There was the scent of game in the air. But they didn't know just what was involved—yet.

"This was after I'd moved back to Winter Haven myself. I liked Florida. Still do, for that matter. And as far as I knew Bob was living in Louisiana. So I decided to come back to Winter Haven. I found a job at a nursing home and was doing all right. I suppose the police found me because I was listed in the telephone book under the name Grantham. Or something. I don't know."

Velboom tried to curb his impatience, wanting first to let the woman get this out in her own way.

"Anyway, I forget exactly when this was, but I got this call from somebody with the Morgan City, Louisiana, Police Department."

"Do you remember who the call was from?" Davenport asked.

Jacquelyn O'Hara shook her head. "He may have said, but I didn't pay any attention. I mean, why should I?"

"Of course."

"Anyway, I suppose he did say who he was. And he asked me was I Mrs. Robert Grantham, and I told him I still was. I mean, we were still legally married at the time. We hadn't lived together for a long time, but we were still married then. And then this Louisiana officer, he said he was sorry to tell me that it looked like my husband had been killed. This body, he said, was found in a motel room there, and the identification, the wallet and everything, belonged to Robert T. Grantham of Winter Haven, Florida.

"Well, I asked him how Bob died, and he said he wasn't sure. The autopsy wasn't complete yet, and there weren't any marks on the, uh, deceased, I think that's what he called it, except for a gunshot wound. But the gunshot looked like it was months old and mostly healed up by then, so it wasn't that that killed him.''

Velboom and Davenport looked at each other. Gun-shot wounds? On a corpse in a Louisiana motel room? What was going on here?

"Anyway, this Louisiana cop—excuse me, this offi-cer—said the photo ID looked like the dead man, but they couldn't really be sure. You know how bad driver's license pictures always are, he said, and of course I did. This Louisiana officer wanted me to come there to Mor-gan City and identify the body for them, since they needed someone who actually knew Bob to look at him and officially say that he was the one who was dead.''

"And did you go?"

"Well, that's kind of the funny thing about this. I didn't want to go, but they said it was really important. So I told them to give me a couple days so I could put things right down here and I'd come to Louisiana.

"Then the very next day, while I was trying to get some things done so I'd be free to leave for a little while, this same officer called back and said he didn't need for me to come.''

"Why is that, Mrs. O'Hara?"

"He said they located another woman in Alabama someplace who also claimed to be married to Bob, and she came over and looked at the body and told them it definitely wasn't Bob Grantham.''

"This other woman . . . ?"

Jacquelyn shrugged. "I don't know. I mean, I wouldn't put it past him to be married to two women at once.''

"Did you ever ask him about that? Later on, I mean?"

"No, I never did. I didn't want to pry. Bob didn't like that. And, anyway, it wasn't like it meant anything to me. We were through a long time before we got around to getting a legal divorce. And Bob, I guess he would have done just about anything to get a woman he really wanted, even if that meant getting married to her when he already was married. It wasn't what he did that counted with him, but whether or not he got what he wanted.''

Davenport and Velboom looked at each other but didn't say anything.

''What was I saying?''

''This other Mrs. Grantham said the body was not Robert T. Grantham.''

''Yes, that's right. She said it wasn't, and the police told me that and hung up.''

''Did he ever tell you what happened in Louisiana that time, Mrs. O'Hara?''

''No. And I never asked him either.''

''You really didn't?''

''I said I didn't.''

''Sorry. When, uh, did all this take place?''

''Sometime in 1984, I think that was. Bob and I were divorced in June of 1985.''

''I think we should talk with Robin Boney for a little while now, Mrs. O'Hara, but I know we'll want to ask you some more questions too, if you don't mind.''

''No, but there is one more thing you should know.'' She stood and went over to a desk pushed against the far wall. Opening the top drawer she removed several Polaroid photographs which she handed to Ray Velboom. They were of a nude woman in various poses. Velboom scanned the pictures trying not to reveal his discomfort. He felt odd looking at them in front of Jackie O'Hara. Shuffling through them quickly to make sure they were of the same female, he inquired about their significance.

''I found those in Bob's house,'' answered Jacquelyn. I went through it the other day to see if I could find any clues to his disappearance and came up with these. I have no idea who she is, though.''

Velboom looked at Davenport. Both agents kept their expressions carefully neutral.

16

They led Robin Boney along slowly and gently, asking nothing that would be intimidating, nothing that would be frightening to her. She could relax here and talk freely.

Yes, she was Bob Grantham's niece. Bob was her mother's brother. She and Bob were close, and her uncle was especially close to Robin's little girl.

Yes, her uncle had some health problems. She told Davenport and Velboom about his fall from the roof the previous year and about his surgeries and difficulty walking afterward. She described his cane, his wheelchair, his habits. He chewed tobacco, smoked a little, drank now and then, but not really to excess.

Women? Well, yes, Bob Grantham liked women. Pretty much any woman, actually. And maybe he could be crude sometimes. But he was charming, too, and a nice man, really. She was close to her uncle. Not too long ago when she was down and out he let her come stay with him. She moved into the house with him and ran errands for him and stuff like that.

Wasn't that the sort of thing his ex-wife Jacquelyn O'Hara did for him? Why did he need both of them to help him with errands and such?

Robin looked toward the floor and hesitated before she answered. She and her uncle had had a falling-out. Sort of. It wasn't anything really serious, mind. Just a little difficulty between them. They had decided—both of them together agreeing about it—that maybe it would be better if Robin moved out again.

The agents let that go for the moment. There wasn't a chance in the world that they would forget about it, though.

"Do you know anything about a time, oh, several years ago, I think this would have been, when your uncle had some difficulty while he was living out of Florida? In Louisiana, I think that was?" Velboom asked.

"You know about that?"

"Tell us what you know about it, please, Robin."

"Just . . . you know."

"Please. Whatever you know. It could be a big help if we can get it all straight in our minds so we don't confuse any of these old incidents with the current, um, situation."

"Well, all right, then." She nodded and steepled her fingertips beneath her chin for a moment while appearing to be in thought, perhaps trying to recall the sequence of events from several years before.

"This would have been . . . I think it was in 1983. Right around then."

"Yes," Velboom said softly, encouragingly.

"I got this call from Judith. . . ."

"From whom?"

"Judith. You know." She glanced toward the back of the house where Jacquelyn O'Hara had gone to wait while the agents were talking with Robin.

"I still don't know. . . ."

"Oh, gosh, I thought you knew. Jackie, that is, Jacquelyn, sometimes goes by the name Judith Delk. I just assumed you knew that."

"It isn't important," Davenport soothed. But his pen was busy.

"Please, go on," Velboom added with a gentle smile.

"Well, anyway, I got this call from Jackie saying the police in Louisiana someplace called and said Bob was dead. Well, I just about freaked. You know? She said they told her his body had been found in some motel room up there, and you can imagine how upset that made me."

Velboom and Davenport nodded dutifully.

"But then not too long after I talked to Jackie, my uncle called. He was at the bus station and wanted me to pick him up."

"Where was this?"

"In Lakeland. He was at the Greyhound station in Lakeland. So I drove over there and got him and brought him back."

"And did he mention anything about a dead man in Louisiana?"

"Yes. I asked him. I mean, there was that call from the police saying he was dead. And then when I picked him up I saw that the tag on his luggage had a different name on it. Bob Duke, the tag said. And later, when he was in the shower, I got curious and looked in his wallet. The identification he had in there was for somebody named Bob Duke. There was a driver's license and everything, and the picture sort of looked a little bit like my uncle Bob. But it wasn't him, of course. So when he came out of the shower, I asked him. I mean, I didn't actually say anything about looking in his wallet. But I asked him about the phone call and the luggage tag and like that."

"And what did he tell you about that?"

"Uncle Bob was always real honest with me, even if he wasn't always with everybody else. We had a real good relationship."

"So, anyway," Robin continued, "he knew that I knew he wasn't any saint and we were always close in spite of that. He didn't have to try and hide anything from me. What he said about that thing in Louisiana was that he and this Bob Duke had gotten involved in some drug deal. He didn't say exactly what, and to tell you the truth, I never asked him about that. He just said that it was a drug deal, and he was supposed to bring some money to Bob Duke at this motel.

"Well, he couldn't get there right when he was supposed to. He was late for some reason. And he found Bob Duke dead in the room there. He figured the people who killed Duke would be after him next because he had the money, and he thought it would be easier to hide if they thought he was the one who was already dead. So he left his ID there with the dead guy and took this Bob Duke's identification. I guess what he was thinking was that since Bob Grantham was the one who was supposed to have the money it would all be all right if they thought Bob Grantham was dead, they wouldn't bother going after Bob Duke then. It had to be something like that, because to this day he uses the name Bob Duke for some things. His telephone, for instance. It's listed in the name of Bob Duke. I know that for a fact because I've seen the bills from the telephone company, and they're made out to Bob Duke, not Bob Grantham."

"And this never struck you as being particularly strange?"

Robin shrugged.

"Did he say who killed Bob Duke or how?"

"No, just that Duke was already dead when my uncle got to that motel room."

"Could Bob Duke have died of natural causes?"

"I wouldn't have any way to know that, would I?"

"No, of course not. Sorry." Davenport smiled. "I wasn't thinking, was I?"

"No problem."

"Did he say what happened to the money he was supposed to deliver to Mr. Duke? This drug money or whatever it was?"

"He never said anything about that. I'd guess he would've kept it. I mean, what with Bob Duke being dead and everything."

"And did he say if that money was his to begin with or maybe his and Bob Duke's? Anything like that?"

"He didn't say. I don't know who the money belonged to."

"So he might have been running from whoever killed Bob Duke—assuming Duke did not die of natural causes, that is—*and* whoever the money belonged to?"

"He said nothing to me about that."

"I see." They skirted round the edges of Bob Duke and the Louisiana drug deal a little longer without learning anything more, then Davenport leaned forward and handed Robin a thin sheaf of Polaroid photographs.

"I hope this won't offend you, Robin, but Jacquelyn gave these to us a little while ago. She said she found them in your uncle's home, but that she doesn't know who the girl is. Perhaps you could help us."

Robin glanced down at the pictures and nodded. "Sure, I knew about these. I mean, I never saw them before. But I've heard about them."

"Oh?"

"Yeah." She laughed. "Sue's boyfriend was really steamed when he heard Bob took these nudie pix." Robin laughed again and handed the photos back to Davenport, obviously unaware of the possible significance of what she'd just told the FDLE agents.

Just how angry had the cuckolded boyfriend been?

17

The photographs Robin held in her hand were of a young blond woman, perhaps in her early twenties, with a stunning body and a high-swept punk hairdo. Most of the pictures were bedroom scenes, deliberately and blatantly provocative and sexy.

"You said this girl's name is Sue?" Davenport asked.

"That's right."

"And her last name?" His pen was poised, ready to jot down the name.

"I don't know that."

Davenport raised an eyebrow.

"I mean, I'm sure she must have told me, but I guess I didn't pay all that much attention. I don't remember what it is," Robin said.

"How well do you know Sue?" Velboom asked.

"Not very. I mean, I know her. Sort of. I introduced her to my uncle. But I don't know her real well."

"Where do you know her from?"

"I met her in the Polk County jail," Robin said without elaboration. Neither Velboom nor Davenport interrupted the flow of the woman's statement. But each made a mental note that this was a comment that would have to be pursued later. "We talked a lot and kind of got along,'' Robin went on without pause. ''Then later on Sue called me. She was complaining about her boyfriend. This guy and her used to get into a lot of arguments, I guess, and he had a temper. She said arguing was one thing, but this time just after we met he beat up on her. She said she had bruises all over and was scared of him. She said she wanted to get away from him but she didn't have a place to go. That's why she called me, to see if I had a place where she could come for a while.

''Well, I didn't. Not at my place, that is. But I thought about my uncle Bob. He had plenty of room. I told her I'd talk to him, and I did, and he said she could come stay there if she wanted. So when Sue got back with me, I told her about Bob. She and him got together, and she moved into his house with him there. Just as a temporary thing to help her out, you understand.''

Robin hesitated a fraction of a second, then seemed to make up her mind about something. ''Sue told me about all this after, so I guess it's okay for me to tell you about it now. I mean, if she didn't want anybody to know she wouldn't have told me. You know?''

Davenport nodded encouragement.

''You already know what my uncle was like. There wasn't any woman hardly that he wouldn't go after, and Sue is awful pretty. You can sure see that for yourselves.'' Robin laughed and glanced down at the photographs that showed all of Sue in the flesh.

''Well, anyway, I don't know if it was right away or after a couple days, but they were both sitting on the couch watching television, and Bob reached over and put his hand on her leg. Sue didn't slap him or anything, so he reached up and grabbed her, uh, you know. Up here.'' Robin motioned to indicate her bosom. ''She said he just took hold and gave her a squeeze. She said she laughed and called him a dirty old man, and that made him grin. Uncle Bob would have thought that was pretty spunky, if you know what I mean.

"And after that they kind of fooled around a little, nothing real serious, just wrestling around and being kind of playful, until Sue got up and said she was going to shower and go to bed. Uncle Bob stayed where he was, but when she got out of the shower a little bit later there was this flashbulb thing going off—that would be this picture here—and he laughed. He was real proud of the picture, too. She said he thought she should be in *Playboy* or something.

"Well, Sue wasn't upset, really. She was real cool. She wrapped a towel around herself and told him she'd like a little privacy. Then when she was done she went into his bedroom—it was as much her idea as his, I guess—and got into bed with him. He took some more pictures and took the last of the roll in the morning. She didn't mind posing for him. And you can bet she told her boyfriend about it after. I think that's one of the reasons she let Bob take those pictures and why she slept with him. She wanted to make the boyfriend jealous."

"Did it work?"

"Yeah, I suppose it did. She only stayed with Bob a little while. Then Sue and her boyfriend patched it up, and she went back to live with him again."

"And you say the boyfriend didn't like knowing that your uncle had these pictures?"

"That's right. After Sue went back with him this guy called my uncle and told him he wasn't to see Sue anymore and that he wanted the pictures Bob had taken of Sue. All of them. I know that part is true for sure, because Bob told me about the phone calls."

"This boyfriend. Do you know his name?"

"Bill. His name is Bill."

"And his last name?"

Robin shook her head. "I don't know."

"Do you know how we can reach either Sue or Bill? A telephone number, where they work, anything like that?"

She shook her head again. "I'm sorry."

Velboom glanced over at Davenport. They didn't have to speak to know what the other was thinking. There definitely were more people in this case that they needed to locate and talk to. And much more that they needed to know. There was Sue's angry boyfriend who had a temper and had a more than good enough reason to vent it on Robert Grantham. And then there was Robin Boney herself. Why had she been in jail when she met Sue to begin with? The more they learned about this case, the more complicated it became.

"There are a few more things we need to know about your uncle, Robin," Steve Davenport said in a gentle, soothing tone of voice.

Robin sighed once, then nodded and leaned forward, attentive to the agents' questions and—at least to outward appearances—eager to help them solve this mystery of her uncle's disappearance.

18

It was time to speak to both women, so the agents had Mrs. O'Hara return.

"Now could either of you tell us anything more about this trip to Las Vegas?" Ray Velboom asked. "Anything at all that you might know about it, in particular anything that strikes you as unusual."

"I can tell you about it some," Jacquelyn O'Hara said. She was sitting at the opposite end of the couch from Robin Boney. "I made the reservations for this trip, just like I did for him occasionally before."

"This was not Robert Grantham's first visit to Las Vegas then?"

"Oh my, no. Bob loved to gamble, almost any kind of gambling, and he was especially fond of Las Vegas. He was there just a few months ago, and when he came back he had this whole bag—one of those small duffel things, I think they call them—full of coins. Mostly quarters, I think. He said he hit a jackpot and was all full of himself, showing off those coins to me and my boyfriend. But then knowing Bob it's just as likely that he stopped at a bank and got some bills changed into quarters so he could show off. With him you never know. But I do know this, he was hardly home from that trip before he was wanting to go again. This time, let me see, he asked me to get him four tickets—"

"Four?"

Jackie O'Hara nodded. "They were supposed to be for Bob, for a golfing friend of his named Les Baker, and two others. He never said who those were for, but I'd guess he had a couple bimbos in mind. Or maybe he thought he could get lucky if he could promise some nice-looking waitress a trip to Las Vegas. Bob is like that, you know."

"And did you get the four tickets?"

Jackie shook her head. "I called the travel agent—" Davenport interrupted her for a moment while he jotted down the name of the travel agency Grantham preferred. "When I told Bob what the tickets would cost he said I should hold off, that he'd get back to me. As it turned out he bought the tickets himself. Just two of them, though. One for him and one for Les. He never said anything about the other two."

"And did he mention any reason why he would fly out of Orlando instead of Tampa?" The question was asked by Ray Velboom. But then Steve Davenport already had an answer for that one.

"It was cheaper to take this particular flight from Orlando than to get one out of Tampa. Besides," Jackie said, "from Winter Haven it's about the same distance to the one as it is to the other, and the Orlando airport is easier to reach. The Orlando airport is on this side of the city, so from here you don't have to go through city traffic to reach it. Tampa's airport is all the way on the far side of the city, and you have to go through a lot of city traffic to get there."

"I see. And, um, was there anything unusual about this trip?"

"Well, there was one thing. But you have to remember that Bob likes to exaggerate things. He likes to be— I suppose you could say—dramatic."

"So keeping that in mind, what happened during this recent trip that you say was unusual?"

"There was a call from Bob. It would have been the day after he left, I think. That would make it—what?— the fifth of May? Yes, I think that was it. Anyway, my boyfriend Ray answered the phone, and it was Bob calling from Las Vegas. He said he was in his hotel—that was the Fremont, he was staying there this time, although he always used to stay at the Four Queens—and that he had locked himself in his room."

"Did he say—?"

"He said he was scared that someone was trying to rip him off. He said he won twenty thousand dollars and had it all in cash, and he was afraid someone was going to try and take it from him."

"Do you know who might have been trying to rip him off?"

"Officer, I don't even know for sure that he'd won twenty dollars, much less twenty thousand. Don't forget, this is Bob Grantham we're talking about here."

"Did he tell you anything else that time?"

"Not really. We didn't talk all that long. He sounded kind of hyped. Excited, like. We talked just a little while and then he wanted to get off the line. Ray and I didn't really take him very seriously at the time. We know Bob better than that."

"I see. And did you hear from him again before he, uh, disappeared?"

"Once. Sort of."

"Sort of?"

"We were out. When we got back there was a message on the answering machine. It was Bob. All he said was that he was sorry he missed catching us but that he'd be home the next day. That was the last thing I've heard from him."

"And since then?"

"You know all about that, I'm sure. When he didn't come home on time, I started looking for him. First, I stopped by the house, but he wasn't there. Then I called the Orlando airport to see if his car left the lot on time."

"Excuse me. You say you called the airport parking garage?"

"That's right."

"How did you know to do that? I mean, most people don't realize how closely the cars in those lots are checked."

"Oh, Bob told me all about how they do that."

"Really? And do you happen to know how he would have been aware of it?"

"Of course. Bob used to work for Budget Car Rental, at both the Orlando and the Tampa airports. He knew all about that stuff."

Velboom gave Davenport a questioning look. Grantham was intimately acquainted with the working procedures at airport parking lots. With the Orlando and Tampa airport lots in particular. Was that significant in relation to the man's disappearance? Or was it merely a smokescreen of coincidence? It seemed too soon to decide. But it was certainly something to be tucked away to be examined later if the facts of the case warranted additional attention.

"Go on, please, Mrs. O'Hara."

"Sure. Anyway, after the man at the Orlando airport said the car had left there all right, and Bob still wasn't home, I called all the hospitals I could think of. And after that I filled out the missing persons report with the Winter Haven Police Department. I didn't hear anything more until I read about the car being found in Tampa. And then, of course, Robin called and told me you were coming to talk with us."

"Can you think of any reason why anyone might want to kill Robert Grantham?" Davenport asked, making no mention of the twenty thousand dollars in cash that the missing man claimed to have in his possession several days before his disappearance.

Jacquelyn O'Hara frowned and pulled back, physically moved backward but also withdrew emotionally from her open cooperativeness. "I really couldn't answer that."

"No?"

"I've been thinking of Bob in terms of his being still alive. I can't think of anyone who would benefit from his death."

"No one?"

"No. No one."

"And you?" Davenport looked at Robin Boney. She merely shook her head.

Shrugging and changing smoothly to a neutral subject, the two FDLE agents began compiling a list of Robert Grantham's friends—golf and poker buddies, girl-friends, employees, and even casual acquaintances—everyone either woman could remember having played a role in Robert Grantham's life.

Among them were Wauchula, Florida, residents Rudy Benton and Maurice Gilliard, both old friends and golfing partners of the missing man. There was Jimmy Abbott, Robin's former husband and member of the Abbott Brothers Band, who could be found at the Club 92 in Seffner. Les Baker, another Wauchula resident. And Rebecca Haislip, Grantham's housekeeper.

"Becky only lives about a mile down the road."

"You say she is Grantham's housekeeper?"

"That's right."

"She might know a lot about his comings and goings, I would presume."

Jackie O'Hara shrugged. "She might."

"Do you happen to know how we could reach her?"

"I have her address and phone number here somewhere. Just a minute, and I'll find it for you."

"You ladies are being a big help. Both of you," Velboom said with an encouraging smile. "We really appreciate this."

"Just find Bob. Okay?"

"We'll do our very best. That much we can promise."

19

After calling to verify that she was at home and would see them, Velboom and Davenport drove straight from Jacquelyn O'Hara's house to the home of Grantham's housekeeper Becky Haislip. They found the woman waiting in her front yard. She did not choose to invite them inside, so they spoke with her in the shade of a moss-strung oak tree.

"Why is it you wanted to talk with me?" she asked.

"We just need to get some information about Mr. Grantham. You do know him, don't you?" Davenport queried.

"Yes, but why . . . ?"

"This really won't take long," Velboom said with a disarming display of charm. "How is it that you came to know Robert Grantham."

"I answered an ad in the newspaper. That would have been this past December."

"And he hired you to do what?"

"I clean for him. His house and his business, too. Of course they're all at the same place together. But I cleaned, like, the office and the rest of the house, too. Twice each week for about three months."

"You don't work for him anymore?"

Becky Haislip shook her head.

"Did you quit or did he fire you?"

"I quit him."

"Would you mind telling us why?"

"If you knew that man you'd know why I didn't want to be around him no more. He wanted me to do things that no decent woman would do. I told him I wasn't like that, but he wouldn't leave be. I hated to lose the job. He paid sixty dollars an hour and the work wasn't hard . . . but some things are more important than money. I quit him . . . oh . . . it would be about six weeks ago now."

"Have you seen him since that time?"

"No, I have not. Don't want to see him again, neither."

Asked about Grantham's trips, Becky Haislip said during the three months she worked for him, Grantham had gone to Las Vegas at least three times.

"He always talked big before he left about how he

was gonna do this and he was gonna do that. He was always gonna win all the money they had out there. I don't recall him talking so big when he got back from any of those trips, though.''

''But he did go on gambling trips frequently?''

''I can't tell you what he did other times, just the times he went while I was working for him. That would have been once a month, more or less.''

''Do you remember anything unusual happening while you worked for him?''

''What do you mean 'unusual'?''

''Strange occurrences, strange visitors, anything out of the ordinary.''

Like Jacquelyn O'Hara and Robin Boney, Becky Haislip was aware of Grantham's sometime use of the name Bob Duke, and she told the investigators about that. She professed not to know anything about any drug dealings or other troubles of Robert Grantham, although Robin Boney had mentioned such things to her on occasion.

''There was the one other thing,'' she said finally. ''But that wasn't when I worked for him. I'd quit him by then.''

''Oh? And what was that?''

''It was a phone call. Collect. It was from a man who said he was Mike Bentley. I don't know anybody by that name but I took the call anyway because of my mother's health. I was afraid it was somebody calling to talk to me about her. That's why I said I'd pay for the call. But all this Bentley said when I gave him my name was that he didn't know me, but did I know a Grantham. I said that I did, and the man hung up. I don't know what any of that was about. I called the operator back, but all she could tell me was that the call came from Michigan. Someplace in Michigan. To tell you the truth, you coming here this evening, I thought maybe it had something to do with that call. Is Bob Grantham in some kind of trouble with the law?''

Davenport told her that the man was missing. She shook her head. ''I don't know. I just don't know about that man.''

They spent a few more minutes discussing Robert Grantham, his habits, likes and dislikes, and any other particulars of the man. The FDLE agents thanked Ms. Haislip and left.

20

It was past eight o'clock in the evening when FDLE special agents Ray Velboom and Steve Davenport left Becky Haislip's residence, and both were more than ready for some supper.

''I know a pretty good place in town here if you trust my judgment,'' Davenport suggested.

''Fine, but would you mind stopping at the first convenience store you see. Or anyplace else that has a public phone for that matter.''

Davenport raised an eyebrow in silent inquiry, and Velboom smiled. ''You didn't see the car and haven't had a chance yet to get into the reports that are piling up, but all three of those women mentioned something, Steve. Something that seems to be missing.''

''The wheelchair,'' Davenport said immediately.

''You did catch it.''

Davenport nodded. "The car inventory shows a cane but no wheelchair. The guy should have had his wheelchair with him on an extended trip like that."

"Exactly. So I think I'll call Sgt. Raley."

"Raley. He's—"

"Tampa International police force."

"Right." Davenport spotted a pay phone outside a convenience market, and he pulled in so Velboom could place a credit-card call to Tampa.

"No, I don't recall a wheelchair being found anywhere near that Thunderbird," Raley said after Velboom identified himself and had posed the question. "But I think there are a couple of them in Lost and Found. Do you know what Grantham's chair looks like?"

Robin Boney, Jacquelyn O'Hara, and Becky Haislip were all in agreement about the wheelchair. "It has a green seat and there is a lot of roofing tar splattered on the metal and smudged on the seat, too."

"Tar?"

"That's the guy's business. Roofing."

"If you say so. I'll look for a wheelchair with tar on it and call you right back."

"We aren't at the office, sergeant. Why don't I give you a buzz back in an hour or so?"

"I'll have your answer then."

"Oh, and Raley . . ."

"Yes?"

"There's one more thing I'd like you to check for me, if you don't mind."

"Not at all. Anything we can do, you know?"

Velboom spoke very briefly and soon disconnected.

"Well?" Davenport asked when Velboom returned to the car.

"He's checking on it now. I'll call back after we've had supper."

Davenport nodded and put the car in gear.

An hour and a half later, and feeling considerably better with a good meal in his stomach, Velboom placed his second call of the evening to Tampa International Airport police sergeant Dan Raley.

"What do you have, sergeant?"

"Two wheelchairs. But neither of them matches the description of Robert Grantham's chair. We have brown, we have black, we have no roofing tar. No joy on this one, sorry."

"Okay, thanks. And the other thing?"

"That was even easier. There were two flights leaving during the early morning hours after Grantham's car checked into the parking lot here. Both were Delta. There was Flight 64 that left at 0105 hours for Miami, and Delta 830 that left here at 0450 for Atlanta with connections to Boston and to Portland, Maine."

"Thanks, Raley. You've been a big help."

"Any time."

When Velboom reported the conversation to Steve Davenport, he added a personal theory that was too vague yet to put into a report, but one which he couldn't ignore.

"The wheelchair, which he needs in order to get around, is missing. And canes are cheap and easy to replace."

"And those Delta flights," Davenport added, quickly catching onto Velboom's line of thought, "mean Mr. Grantham, wheelchair included, could easily have slipped off to any place in the country without anyone being the wiser. Or for that matter, especially if he really did have twenty thousand in cash in his hip pocket, by now he could be quite literally anywhere in the world."

"Which raises the interesting possibility that maybe our friend Grantham isn't a murder victim after all—but just could be a murderer instead."

21

Early Saturday morning Ray Velboom dialed information in search of the number of McLeod Trucking in Wauchula, Florida. The operator told him the closest she could come was McLeod Harvesting and Hauling. Hoping for the best, Velboom first called the trucking company to get directions to it, then called Steve Davenport.

"I'll pick you up on my way down," he told the Polk County agent.

"I'll be ready."

Wauchula is in Hardee County, about forty miles south of Davenport's base in Lakeland, located on US 17 in the heart of Florida's citrus and cattle producing country. From Tampa it took Velboom, picking up Davenport on the way, about an hour and a half to reach the small, normally quiet town.

B.D. McLeod, the owner of McLeod Harvesting and Hauling, was in and readily agreed to see the FDLE agents. He could not help them locate Les Baker at that particular moment, though, because Baker was on the road. McLeod asked if he might be able to help.

"We're investigating the disappearance of a man named Bob Grantham. Do you know him?"

"I know him. Not well, I wouldn't say, but I know

him. He's a friend of Les's. I heard he was missing. You're hoping Les might know something about it, right?''

''Naturally we want to talk with Mr. Baker to see if he might have information that would be helpful. Do you know about any plans Mr. Baker and Bob Grantham might have made recently?''

''I know about a trip to Las Vegas they planned,'' McLeod said, rising to the bait Velboom had placed in front of him.

''Really? Tell us about that, please.''

''That's just about all I know. They intended to take a trip out there together. Les asked me for the time off, and it was fine with me. Then at the last minute we had some deliveries come up that just couldn't be put off, and I told Les he'd have to make it some other time. I really needed him for this job. And Les is a good man. Reliable. He's been driving for me about seven years now, I think it is. I needed him, so he told Grantham he couldn't make the Vegas trip. Otherwise he would have been with Grantham on that trip.''

''And do you know where he was during that period, say from May 4 through May 8?''

''He was up north. Michigan. Would you like to see his travel vouchers?''

The agents were quick to accept McLeod's offer.

McLeod's secretary found the paperwork and gave it to her boss, who in turn passed it over to Velboom and Davenport.

The itinerary indicated that on April 27, Les Baker picked up a load in Houston, Texas, and dropped it off in Miami on May 4. That same day he reloaded in Pompano and Homestead and headed north to Brighton, Michigan, arriving there on May 8.

While Bob Grantham was in Las Vegas enjoying himself—or perhaps fearfully hiding from a party or parties unknown, depending on whether one wanted to believe his telephone call to Jacquelyn O'Hara—Les Baker was in the cab of his truck driving north on Interstate 75. And on the date when Grantham flew back to Orlando and for some reason took his car to the Tampa airport, Les Baker was a thousand miles away.

Davenport looked over the paperwork and asked, "Why did it take Baker so long to get from Houston to Miami?"

"He stopped in Zolfo Springs to play in a golf tournament that weekend. He cleared it with me beforehand." Zolfo Springs is a charming, Old South town on the Peace River a few miles south of Wauchula. McLeod smiled and added, "Otherwise I probably wouldn't know about it to tell you. Come to think of it, if I remember correctly, it was Bob Grantham who was Les's partner in that tournament."

"I see."

"I guess that would be the last time Les saw Bob, because Les went on the road right after and Grantham went on to Las Vegas. Les told me when he called in one day on that run that he'd talked to a mutual friend of theirs and heard that Grantham hadn't returned from Las Vegas, that he was missing, something about his car being found someplace. Which brings us to you gentlemen and the reason for your visit here."

"How did Baker sound when he told you this?"

"Shocked. Very upset. They're friends. You know?"

"Yes, of course."

The agents spoke with B. D. McLeod a little longer without learning anything of significance. Les Baker was a trustworthy employee in McLeod's opinion and a good man. McLeod professed not to know Robert Grantham well enough to have an opinion about him.

And no, for the record, he had no idea where Grantham was or what might have happened to him.

22

Wanting to zero in on the character of the missing man after what his ex-wife and niece told them, Velboom and Davenport decided they should talk to some of Grantham's employees, both past and present, and in particular the female employees. They decided to start with two on the list Jaquelyn O'Hara had given them, for the expedient reason that the two women shared an apartment. Taking a chance on finding one or both of the women at home, the agents drove there without calling ahead. They were lucky.

A young woman cracked open the front door of the apartment. A flimsy chain prevented her from opening it completely. The only thing the two agents could see was her face and a mop of tousled hair.

"Yes?" she asked suspiciously.

"Are you Kim Edwards or Tressa Brantley?"

The girl nodded but did not indicate which one she was. Instead she closed the door a bit more.

Ray Velboom produced his badge and held it for her to see. He introduced himself and Steve Davenport.

"We're with the Florida Department of Law Enforcement, and we'd like to talk to you about a Robert Grantham. I believe you know him."

70

"Oh, yeah. I remember reading in the paper about him being missing. Weird, huh? Did you find out what happened to him?"

"Not yet. That's why we're here. We'd like to ask you some questions."

The girl's eyes widened. "Hey, you don't think I had anything to do with him being missing, do you?"

"No, of course not," Velboom said in his soothing best. "We just want to do some follow-up questions and fill out what we've heard about the man. That's all."

She still looked uncertain so Velboom took a more stern stance with her. "We need to talk with you. Right now," he insisted.

Reluctantly she closed the door, disengaged the meager safety chain and opened it again. "Come on in."

The agents went inside and helped themselves to seats without waiting to be asked. The girl joined them. She looked nervous.

"How can I help you?" she asked.

"You can start by telling us your name."

"Kim Edwards."

"We understand you worked for Grantham?"

"Yes. I started . . . I think it was in August of last year. He was recovering from a bad fall off a roof. My roommate worked for him, and she got me the job. I only worked there for about a week, though."

"Why so short a time?" Davenport asked.

Kim made a face and said, "Man, if you knew this guy you'd have figured that out. The jerk kept coming on to me. Can you believe he actually offered me money to sleep with him? I told him to get lost. You know what he did? He upped the ante. He said he'd take me on an all-expenses-paid trip if I went to bed with him." Again she made a face and pretended to shudder. "God, he was disgusting. He finally told me I had to either put out or get fired. I didn't wait for him to fire me. I quit."

Before either of the agents had time to say anything

the door swung open, startling Velboom, who jumped to his feet. Which in turn startled the young woman who was standing in the front doorway. She let out a shrill, piercing yelp.

"It's okay, Tress. Don't be scared. These guys are the police."

Tressa Brantley and Ray Velboom each stood motionless for a moment as if afraid that if one moved the other would be spooked into flight. After a moment Velboom cleared his throat and, mildly embarrassed, asked Tressa to join them. She closed the door and did so; she was hesitant but willing.

Kim performed introductions. "Tress is the one who got me the job with Bob Grantham," she added.

Velboom expanded on Kim's explanation of who they were and what they wanted.

"Kim and I talked about it after we read about Bob in the papers," Tressa Brantley said. "About what might have happened to him. We couldn't believe it, somebody we know disappearing like that."

The agents allowed the conversation to go on in that innocuous vein for a few minutes to let Tressa become comfortable. Then Davenport began gently steering the talk back in the direction he and Velboom desired. "Kim told us you worked for Grantham last year and that you got her a job with him, too?"

"Yeah."

"What did you do for Grantham?"

"Sometimes I worked in the office. Other times I went out on jobs as a laborer on one of the roofing crews. Whatever was needed at the time."

"How long did you work for him?"

"Let's see . . . he hired me just before he had his accident, whenever that was. And I quit the same time as Kim did. That would have been in August."

"Your roommate told us why she left," Davenport said with a look in Kim's direction as if to affirm the statement. "Did you leave for the same reason?"

"Not exactly. I quit because she did. He hit on me too, but we never did anything."

"Do you have any idea what might have happened to him?" Velboom asked.

"Not really."

"You said a minute ago that the two of you talked about what could have happened. What sort of things did you think of when you did that?"

Tressa looked at Kim, then back at Velboom. "It doesn't mean anything, of course, but I did hear another girl at the place, at the roofing company I mean, talk a couple times about what an easy mark Bob would make."

"How so?"

"Well, for one thing, he always carried a lot of money around with him. He liked cash. You know? And this girl said he'd be an easy target if somebody wanted to rob somebody. But then she was always talking like that. Tough, you know. This same girl told me if Bob ever tried to touch her she'd blow him away. And she had a gun too. I think it was a .22."

"And Bob Grantham. Did he have a gun?"

"Not that I ever saw."

"This girl you heard talking, what is her name?"

"Look, I didn't go to get anybody in trouble. She was just talking, you know? She wasn't serious. I knew her. Really."

"I understand that. What's her name?"

"Shirley. Shirley Lane."

"Do you know where we can reach her?"

"No, I haven't seen her since Kim and I quit last year."

"Anything else either of you can tell us that you think might help?"

There was not much. Both had seen Grantham drink but neither ever saw him drunk. Yes, both knew of other women who worked for him who had, for one reason or another mostly having to do with extra income, agreed to sleep with Grantham. No, neither knew anything about the disappearance other than the little they had read in the newspaper.

And, oh yes, there was that stuff with Robin. But then surely they knew all about that.

About what?

Why, about Robin Boney stealing the checks from Grantham and him filing criminal charges against her, that's what?

Criminal charges? What criminal charges?

Kim and Tressa didn't know all the details. But what they understood was that Robin had forged seven checks belonging to Bob's Insulated Roofing. Robin was supposed to have spent some time in jail before she bonded out. But the police would know more about that then they did, wouldn't they?

Well, yes. Of course they would. Velboom and Davenport were both busy making notes.

The agents thanked Kim Edwards and Tressa Brantley and left. It was interesting, they thought, that people who knew Grantham thought of him as a potential mark for a robbery attempt.

The conversation with Edwards and Brantley shifted the agents' focus once again away from Grantham as murderer and back toward him as victim.

But either could yet prove to be true.

"Are you ready to quit for the day?" Velboom asked.

"Not unless you want to."

"How would you like to go jukin'? Say, to this Club 92 place where Robin Boney's ex works."

"That sounds good to me."

23

Seffner, and the Club 92, are located just east of Tampa on U.S. highway 92 which once was the principal east-west route through central Florida. Since the coming of the interstate system and I-4 linking Tampa with Orlando and Daytona Beach, much of U.S. 92 has degenerated into a seedy strip of sunbaked neglect.

Despite that, Velboom and Davenport found Club 92 enjoying about as much business as the limitations of space would permit. They found a parking place out in the weeds and hiked to the front door. Going inside was like walking into a pool of tepid gelatin. The combined noise of music and merriment seemed a physical presence through which they waded.

The music came from a stage tucked into a corner to the left of the door. The band's drummer was thumping out a marrow-deep rhythm on a bass drum, which had the name "The Jimmy Abbott Band" stenciled on its vibrating skin.

The place smelled of beer and cigarette smoke. Velboom pushed his way through the crowd to the bar with Steve Davenport close on his heels.

As much by way of sign language as actual speech the agents each ordered a beer, and then settled in to nurse their drinks until the band's next break.

Less than twenty minutes later the band completed their set, and the dancers retired to their tables for a drink in anticipation of another frenzy on the dance floor.

Velboom and Davenport asked a band member to point out Robin Boney's former husband, and then introduced themselves to the enthusiastic Abbott, who was still "up" with the excitement of his music.

"Lying Bob Grantham? Sure I know him. I used to be married to his niece, you know."

"So we understand, Mr. Abbott."

The musician grinned. "Jimmy. Everybody calls me Jimmy."

"All right, Jimmy. Would you mind telling us about this Robert Grantham, please?"

"Like where he is? Man, I don't know that. I heard he disappeared, but I don't know nothing about that."

"No, I mean more like what sort of person Grantham is."

"Oh, that." Abbott shrugged. "The guy's a schemer and a con man, that's what he's like. I wouldn't trust him or anything he says. Not for anything important, I wouldn't. I mean, he'd come in here lots. Come in and flash a wad of cash and try to pick up chicks. Any old bag, really. He'd start off hitting on the young stuff, but if he couldn't get anything prime, he'd settle for whatever he could get. I mean, man, this guy was a regular pervert. He pissed off a lot of people, too. The way he acted and everything."

"How angry did these people get?"

"PO'd. But not, like, violent or anything, if that's what you mean."

"That's what we mean, all right."

"Naw, Bob wasn't worth getting that mad at. He was just a sort of dirty old man."

"I understand he was close to your ex-wife."

"Yeah. They used to be, anyhow. Until he had Robin put in jail. They weren't so awful close after that. Which you can understand. You know?"

"Tell us about that." Robin Boney herself had mentioned being in jail, just a casual comment that she gave no particular weight or emphasis. And her friends Kim Edwards and Tressa Brantley had mentioned the incident too.

"I don't really know the details. That was after Robin and me split. I think it had something to do with her writing checks on Bob's bank account. You know. Something like that."

They spoke with Abbott a little longer, but the band leader said he knew nothing about where Grantham might be or about anyone who might want to cause serious harm to the man.

"I mean, the guy is a jerk, but I don't think anyone around here would want to see him done in."

"And do any other band members know him?"

By way of an answer Abbott summoned the band's young and pretty lead singer. "Guys, this is Debbie Ware. She knows Bob. And, look, I'm sorry, but I've forgot your names."

The FDLE agents introduced themselves and went through with Debbie Ware pretty much the same conversation they had just had with Jimmy Abbott. With, predictably, pretty much the same result.

"Sure, I know Bob. He's a liar, a cheat, and a dirty old man. He likes to come in here and hit on any woman that will stand still long enough for him to flash a roll in front of her. He always sweet-talks the ladies, but I'll tell you something. Any of them he can get to put out for him it's because he's paid for the privilege. I can't see any woman hitting the sheets with an old guy like that unless he pays."

"Did he ever try to, um, date you?"

Ware rolled her eyes. "Did he try? Only all the time.

I bet he called me at home a dozen, two dozen times. Whoever gave that creep my phone number is just lucky I don't know who they are, because I'd give them what for, I promise you.''

"I take it that you never went out with him then?''

"Mister, there isn't that much money in Florida to make me want to get close to that.''

"Do you know of anyone who might feel so strongly about Grantham that they would want to cause him harm?''

"I know what you're getting at, and I'd have to say no, I don't. I mean, I know a lot of people, guys and girls, too, who might want to haul off and sock him one. Or give him a good kick where he'd feel it the most. But nothing more than that. Look, we're running past time to start our next set. Do you need me for anything more?''

"No. If you think of anything . . .''

"Sure, you bet.''

The agents distributed their cards to Abbott and Ware, just in case (and escaped from the asylum scant seconds ahead of the next explosion of frolicking good times). They could feel more than hear the deep, driving thuds of that bass drum even when they were back into the cool, clean, refreshing night air outdoors.

24

Come Monday morning the FDLE agents wanted to look into the records on Robin Boney's arrest and incarceration. Though, Ray Velboom thought he should do some routine housekeeping chores relating to the case.

While still in the Tampa office, he entered Robert T. Grantham's name and description in the missing persons category of the Florida Crime Information Center and National Crime Information Center (FCIC/NCIC) computer network. Once that was done, any police department in the country, at least in theory, would be flagged with a message to contact the FDLE Tampa office if Grantham or anyone answering his description were located—dead or alive.

And while he was at it, Velboom used the same computer network to request a criminal background check on the missing man.

Lying Bob Grantham was not altogether unknown to the computer. The list of convictions that came back included:

3/13/51   Rape—committed to School for Boys
8/27/53   Armed Robbery—5 years in prison

4/9/57	Impersonating an officer and Extortion—3 years in prison
1/30/61	Robbery—disposition unknown
7/28/65	Bad checks—disposition unknown
1/12/68	Assault and Battery—disposition unknown
5/1/76	Failure to redeliver a Hired Vehicle—2 years probation

Bob Grantham, it seemed, was not a particularly nice man.

More to the point, based on past performance, it seemed entirely possible that Grantham had the potential to have committed whatever crime took place inside that abandoned Ford Thunderbird.

He might well have been the victim. But then again he could as easily prove to be the perpetrator. Velboom's task, and Davenport's, was to find out which. And then see what could be done about it.

Velboom left the computer terminal in the FDLE Tampa office and headed for Lakeland to pick up Steve Davenport.

25

The two agents drove from Lakeland to Winter Haven rather than dropping straight south to the county seat in Bartow. Their first stop of the day was at the Central Travel Agency, where Jacquelyn O'Hara said Grantham bought his tickets for the Las Vegas trip.

After identifying themselves to travel agent Chris Kirsh, Velboom and Davenport asked to see the agency's records of Robert Grantham's travel, in particular his recent trip west.

On April 29 Grantham purchased two one-way tickets for the westward leg of the trip and two separate one-way tickets for the return portion. Grantham's name was to be on one set of tickets and the name Les Baker on the other.

The two men were scheduled to leave Orlando International at 9:30 A.M. Monday, May 4, on Continental flight 875 and arrive in Denver, Colorado, around 11:30 A.M. Mountain Time. From Denver's Stapleton Airport they were to take Continental flight 1065, leaving at 2:35 P.M. and arriving in at Las Vegas's McCarran Field at 3:25 P.M. Pacific Time.

Each one-way ticket cost $140. Grantham's included a special condition that a wheelchair be made available for him at Stapleton Airport in Denver and another for use within the airport terminal at McCarran in Las Vegas.

At the same time the westbound tickets were obtained, Grantham booked return flights via TranStar Airlines flight 898 departing Las Vegas at 7:25 A.M. on Thursday, May 7, en route to a stopover in Houston until 1:15 P.M., when they would board TranStar flight 534 for a return to Orlando at 4:30 P.M. As is the usual practice with airline ticketing, all times stated were local.

The one-way return tickets each cost $139 and also included wheelchair requests for Grantham. Bob Grantham paid for all four tickets with a single check made out to the travel agency.

When asked why Grantham flew out of Orlando instead of Tampa and used a combination of one-way flights rather than round-trip ticketing, Miss Kirsh explained that the customer had asked for the cheapest possible fares. The itinerary she put together for him proved to be the least expensive she could devise. The customer had been willing to fly out of either Tampa or Orlando; cost-cutting was of more importance to him than the choice of airport.

Asked if she could describe the customer, Miss Kirsh thought for a moment, then said, "He had grayish hair and a beard. And he walked with a cane. About fifty years old, I would say. He seemed like a nice man."

From the travel agency, the FDLE agents visited the Polk County State Attorney's Office and spoke with prosecutor Brad Copley so that they could arm themselves with a subpoena—a necessity when dealing with medical records—and drove to the Winter Haven hospital, where Robert Grantham had been treated for his injuries after his fall from the roof.

The blood found smeared so thick throughout the missing man's Thunderbird tested as Type A, and determining if this was a match with Grantham's blood type was a logical and necessary step.

The hospital files though, incredibly enough, failed to record Grantham's blood type even though he had undergone several surgeries there. For some reason the information was missing.

Disappointed, Velboom and Davenport headed for Bartow and the courthouse where, hopefully, Robin Boney's records should be available.

26

Criminal case reports are a matter of public record and can be viewed by anyone, so Velboom and Davenport did not even have to show their credentials in order to secure Robin Boney's court file. A clerk at the Polk County courthouse needed only minutes to find the requested file and hand it over to the agents.

The original affidavit of complaint was filed early in August 1986, by Detective Sgt. John McKinney of the Bartow Police Department, acting on information provided by Robert Grantham of Winter Haven. According to the police report, Grantham discovered the problem when his bank notified him that his business checking account was overdrawn.

When he tried to balance the account, Grantham found that several checks were missing from the office in his home. Those checks had been filled out and cashed as payroll checks, all at banks in Bartow.

After recovering the stolen checks from Grantham's

bank, Bartow identification specialist Sgt. David Brooks processed the checks for fingerprints, and came up with a usable latent print on the back of check number 146.

The fingerprint proved to be the left middle finger of Robin Abbott, also known as Robin Boney, who had been living at Grantham's home—where the business office was also located—ever since Grantham's accident.

In late August, according to the report, Sgt. McKinney confronted Robin Boney and told her there was fingerprint evidence to show that she was the party who forged the payroll checks drawn against her uncle's business.

She then admitted taking the business checks, but insisted that Grantham had given her permission to cash them for her own personal use.

Four days later Grantham was interviewed again, and once again denied giving her, or anyone else, permission to take the checks or to cash them. He also confirmed that his niece had access to the business office while she was living in the house with him.

For reasons not made clear in the official file, a felony warrant was issued against Robin Boney but was not served until January 1987.

A pretrial conference was held on March 20, 1987, nearly a month and a half before Grantham's disappearance, and a plea bargain was reached between Robin Boney's assistant public defender and the prosecutor who was assigned to the case. On that date she entered a plea of guilty to four counts of grand theft, and in exchange the state dropped eight counts of forgery.

There was no mention in the file of what sentence had been agreed to. Velboom and Davenport assumed punishment was to be left up to the judge who would hear disposition of the case, which was scheduled for April 30, the Thursday before Robert Grantham was to travel to Las Vegas.

Although they knew better than to second-guess the

action a judge might choose to take, both agents were aware that Robin Boney—divorced and with a child to care for—faced a potential sentence that could send her into the state correctional system for several years.

And on Monday, April 27, Robin Boney's attorney filed a request that the sentencing date be postponed. The court obliged by resetting the hearing for June 4.

Both agents found themselves asking the same question: Was there anything significant in Robin Boney's request for a continuance of her sentencing?

Her plea had already been entered, and all the dealing presumably was over and done with. Yet at the last minute, just before her loving uncle—who was also the complaining party in the grand theft case against her— took a vacation, she suddenly wanted to delay the hearing.

Was there a connection? Did Robin Boney have reason to believe that things would go easier for her if Grantham were not present to testify against her? More to the point, did Robin Boney have reason to believe that Grantham would not be able to speak against her if a delay was granted?

It was, Davenport and Velboom conceded, something to think about.

27

No investigator can ever really anticipate the things he will learn in a case or the way he will learn them. Some people, in an effort to be helpful, will call attention to the smallest of details. And others, even if genuinely wanting to be of help, may overlook the most glaringly vital pieces of information. As for the investigators, they never know which of those extremes they may be facing at any given moment. Nor can they always know what will or will not turn out to be important. The best the investigator can do is to follow up on every scrap of information that becomes available and hope for the best. Nothing was too insignificant to pursue.

But in truth there are times when the effort seems hardly worth the return.

The morning after the trip to Bartow, Steve Davenport received a call at his Lakeland office from Detective William McNally of the Winter Haven Police Department.

"A woman from Haines City contacted me, Davenport. I suppose she called us instead of you because this Grantham fellow is from Winter Haven. For whatever it's worth, she says she has some information about your guy Grantham."

"Good, let's follow up on it."

"Would you like me to go with you to see her? I can call her back and set it up if you want."

"That sounds good to me. The quicker the better. Let me know the time, and I'll come by and pick you up."

"I'll get right back to you."

While McNally was calling back the informant, Davenport got on the phone to Ray Velboom to see if he wanted to go along as well; he did.

Davenport and Velboom drove by the Winter Haven Police Department in plenty of time to get McNally and follow the Winter Haven detective's directions to the residence of Richard and Ann Eglin. It was Mrs. Eglin who had spoken to McNally earlier.

The Eglins lived in a tidy mobile home community in the northeastern Polk County town of Haines City, winter home of the Kansas City Royals baseball team. The couple invited the FDLE agents and local detective inside and made them comfortable. Mrs. Eglin insisted on preparing iced tea for the visitors.

"Two years ago, spring of 1985 that would have been, we needed a new roof on our mobile. We hired Bob's Insulated Roofing to do the job. We chose them because we'd seen them doing some other roofs in the park here, and it seemed like they did a nice job. That's how we met Bob."

"Grantham?"

"That's right. He's the Bob in Bob's Insulated Roofing, isn't he?"

"Yes, I suppose he is."

"Of course. Well, anyway, that's how we knew him. He did the work for us—did it just fine—and we didn't see him again until early this May, sometime in the first few days of the month that would have been."

Davenport's interest went up a notch. Work done two years previously didn't excite him much. But now Mrs. Eglin was talking about the period immediately before

Grantham left on his trip to Las Vegas. Perhaps she had something to say after all.

"He came by in the evening about five. I'm sure it was about then because Dick goes to work at five-thirty and he hadn't left yet. Had you?"

Eglin obediently agreed that he had indeed been home at the time, and he, too, saw Robert Grantham that day early in May.

"He came by to pick up a check from us. Not from us, that is, but from one of our neighbors. Bob did some work for her, but she had to go back up north and couldn't stay to see the work done and give him his check. So she asked us to hold the check for her and give it to Bob when the work was all done. Bob told her that would be fine by him, and he came by here that day to get his money."

"I made sure the neighbor's work was all done before I gave him the check, of course," Eglin put in.

"What I thought you should know, after I read in the paper about his car being found, you see, was something he mentioned to us when he was here that day."

"Oh? And what would that have been?"

"When he was here he mentioned that he was about to take a trip."

"Yes?" And so Grantham had been, of course.

"He said he was on his way to Houston."

"Houston?"

"That's right. He said he had to go there for surgery of some kind."

The investigators thanked the Eglins for their time and their help and headed back toward Winter Haven, disappointed.

"Surgery, hell. He was off to play and was just looking for a little sympathy in the meantime."

"Three guys, couple hours of our time apiece, and that's what we get for it."

"Good thing this is a salaried job and not piecework, isn't it?"

Even so, later that day, when FDLE special agent William Miles in the Tampa office asked Velboom if there was anything he could do to help with the Grantham investigation, Velboom asked if he knew anything about airline records and procedures.

"Some. I suppose I can find out whatever I don't know. Why?"

"Oh, I was just wondering if it's possible to find out if Grantham made a trip, or planned one, to Houston that we don't know about."

"What was the name of the airline he used?"

"TranStar," Velboom replied, and Miles grinned. "I'll see what I can find out and get back to you."

True to his word, Miles stopped by Velboom's desk not long afterward. "A lady named Pat Redmon ran Grantham through their computer for me. Grantham did go to Houston, but only as a stop en route from Vegas to Orlando on May 7. He ticketed through and shows up on their computer as making the Houston to Orlando leg of the flight right on schedule. They got into Orlando on time at four-thirty in the afternoon. No way he had any surgery there. Not even if the hospital set up an annex at the airport for pass-through business. You know, those last-minute elective surgeries that you might want to have done while your flight is delayed. There wasn't any time for it."

Velboom sighed. But then this was what he had expected to begin with. There was no point in feeling disappointed that he was proven right. "Thanks, Bill. I appreciate your help."

28

Since a good many of Robert Grantham's close friends were from Wauchula, the small town where earlier they spoke with trucking company owner B. D. McLeod, FDLE agents Velboom and Davenport decided to make another return trip. For the sake of convenience, they asked the local police to cooperate to the extent of loaning the agents a place where they could talk with Grantham's friends. Then they called ahead to set up appointments with Grantham cronies Rudy Benton and Maurice Gilliard. Both had been mentioned by Grantham's ex-wife Jacquelyn O'Hara as being particularly close friends of the missing man.

The Wauchula, Florida, police station proved to be a picturesque white one-story structure that looks like a Florida cracker home that has been converted to official use. It even has a tin roof that extends to form an overhang, beneath which the local police can sit in the shade when on break or take shelter from the near-daily afternoon rains.

The agents arrived early and visited with several of the Wauchula officers, waiting for Rudy Benton to arrive. Then the conversation was taken to an empty office where Ray Velboom commandeered the one comfortable chair in the room, an executive chair behind the lone desk, while Steve Davenport and their witness made do with the considerably less comfortable straightback chairs placed across from the senior investigator.

Benton opened the conversation with the surmise that while he didn't know what they wanted to see him about, he supposed it would be regarding Bob Grantham. Before either agent had time to begin questioning him, Benton said that he would be glad to cooperate any way he could, but that he really did not know anything beyond the obvious fact that Bob was missing.

"Anything you can tell us could prove to be helpful, Mr. Benton. You may not know where he is now, but perhaps you could tell us about his habits, his likes and dislikes . . . you never know what will prove to be helpful in a situation like this."

"Okay, then. Let's get it straight, I suppose I should tell you my real name isn't Rudy, it's David. But everybody calls me Rudy, and you should, too. No need for 'mister' with me."

"That will be fine"—Velboom smiled—"Rudy."

"I met Bob . . . it's been . . . oh . . . about a year ago, I'd say. We met through a mutual friend named Ben Whitacker."

Benton and Bob Grantham began playing golf together on what became pretty much a regular basis. It was their custom—it was all right to say this, wasn't it? the agents weren't going to cause any trouble, were they?—to place a, um, small, only small, wager on the golf games.

Benton liked Grantham for the most part, although Bob could be obnoxious at times. Bob was something of a blowhard—loud and overbearing. He liked to flash large wads of cash in public, particularly where waitresses and barmaids could see, and he would hit on the ladies very crudely—and not too successfully. Rudy didn't much care for that about Bob, or about his constant bragging that he could, did, or had bedded this girl or that one, how practically every female they saw was hot to get into bed with him, and how he was always right on the verge of making hugely improbable sums of money.

"Everybody called him LBG, you know. Lyin' Bob Grantham, that was him. I don't think anybody took him very serious, though. I tell you one thing most of the guys liked about LBG. That's how he was always grabbing for the check and dragging out that wad of his. He was just showing off, paying for drinks and meals like he always did, but it was like he really wanted to do it, so I guess we just kinda let him."

There were other times, though, when the blustering LBG could turn serious and be a genuinely good friend, too. Like when Rudy lost his job as a fence-post salesman because he was having medical problems. He had a kidney transplant and just couldn't keep up with the demands of his work any longer, so he had to quit. When Bob Grantham found out Rudy was unemployed, Bob created a part-time position for him at the roofing company, very light work running errands."

"Tell us what you know about his trip to Las Vegas," Velboom prompted. "You did know about it, I presume."

"I heard Bob talking about it with Les Baker. He's another friend of Bob's, you know."

"Yes, thank you."

"That would have been . . . oh . . . in April, maybe. They were talking about making the trip together. Les couldn't make it, though. Something to do with his work. So Bob went alone."

"When was the last time you saw or heard from him?" Steve Davenport asked.

"Last time I talked with Bob was while he was in Vegas."

"Oh?" Davenport assumed this would be a rehash of the story Grantham gave about locking himself in his room and being afraid to go out again. It was not.

Grantham bragged to his friend about winning a $2,500 jackpot on a slot machine and another $700 playing blackjack.

"I didn't believe him. I mean, I know how Bob is. He's the salt of the earth in a lot of ways, but you can't believe a word the man says. So I didn't make a fuss about him supposed to've won all that money, and I think that kind of disappointed him. He changed the subject then."

Presumably the reason the call was made to begin with, Benton said, was Grantham wanting Rudy to talk to Maurice Gilliard and make sure Maurice had Bob's van ready by the time Bob got home. Maurice was supposed to be doing some work on the roofing company van while Bob was away, and Bob wanted Rudy to make sure the job was complete and on time.

"And that's the last time you talked with Grantham?"

"Yes, I never . . . no, wait a second, I did so talk to him once more after that call."

"Oh?"

"Sure. I spoke to him again . . . it would've been May 7."

"Pardon me?" Velboom sat bolt upright in his chair. Davenport had been idly chewing on the end of a toothpick. It very nearly dropped out of his mouth.

May 7 was the day Grantham returned, or was supposed to return, from Las Vegas.

"Are you *sure* it was the seventh?" Davenport asked, trying to hide his intense interest in Benton's response.

"Sure, I'm sure. He called me about nine, nine-thirty that evening. He was calling from the airport in Orlando. Said he just got in from Las Vegas and was on his way to pick up his luggage. He told me he won forty-two hundred dollars this trip. We talked about that and talked about a golf date for that weekend. He wanted to know what tee time we had. We weren't done talking when the call was cut short. I couldn't tell if the operator cut us off or the phone went dead or what. Anyway, I thought he'd call back, but he didn't. That would have been the last time I talked with him. And, of course, he never showed up for our golf game.''

Velboom thought Benton seemed genuinely sad about the disappearance of his friend. But that hardly seemed important. The question in Velboom's mind, and in Davenport's, was what happened to Lyin' Bob Grantham between the time he spoke with his friend Rudy Benton and the time early that next morning when Tampa Airport Authority meter maid Ester Wolf entered Grantham's car onto her inventory.

During that period, Velboom thought, a telephone was not the only thing that seemed to have gone dead.

And there was something in what Rudy Benton was telling them that didn't seem to fit. Velboom couldn't put a finger on whatever it was. Probably nothing. And he was getting lost now while Steve Davenport continued to talk with the witness.

''. . . talked with Les Baker after that,'' Benton was saying. ''This would have been around the twenty-second, I think. Les was on the road. I told him about Bob disappearing—it was in the papers by then, that's how I heard about it—and Les was as surprised as I was. I mean, we were all playing together in a tournament just the weekend before he went off to Las Vegas, and Les was supposed to have gone with him. Then he up and disappears like that.'' Benton looked toward the ceiling and then down toward the toes of his shoes. He cleared his throat and seemed just a little uncomfortable, although up until then he had been quite calm and relaxed.

Ray Velboom leaned forward and, in a tone that suggested they were all in this together and anything known by one of them should be shared by all, asked, ''What do you think, Rudy? What's your personal opinion about it?''

"I think . . . look, I like Bob. You know?"

"Of course. But if he's in trouble, you want to help him, don't you?"

"Yeah, well, if Bob is in trouble it could be of his own making. You know what I mean?"

"I'm not sure I do, Rudy. And don't worry. We understand that this is just talk. Just thinking out loud."

"Yeah, well, what I really think is that Bob might be up to some scam or something. I mean, I don't know that. But it's the sort of thing he might do, for whatever reasons of his own. And if he did set this up, I think he'll show up again sooner or later."

"Why do you think he would turn up again if he's disappeared deliberately?"

"Because of the insurance settlement that's coming to him, of course. Bob wouldn't turn his back on that kind of money."

It was the second time Velboom and Davenport were caught off guard by Rudy Benton's comments. They hadn't heard anything before about an insurance settlement, and were quick to ask about it.

"Sure. He was supposed to get a hundred thousand dollars as a settlement of his claim for when he fell off that roof last year. The time he busted up his legs? You do know about that, don't you?"

"Yes, we know about that."

"Right. Well, Bob, he filed a claim. And they're supposed to settle up a hundred grand worth. No way the LBG I know is going to walk away from that kind of money, no matter what reason he could have had for faking a disappearance. Mark my words, comes the time for that money to be paid, Bob Grantham will be there to collect it. You just mark my words."

"Yes, uh, thanks. Really."

A hundred thousand dollars. That would seem an awfully good reason to *not* disappear. Wouldn't it? Velboom thought.

29

Maurice Gilliard was already waiting for them outside when the agents finished talking with Rudy Benton. They escorted Gilliard into the borrowed office and completed the introductions.

"As you probably already guessed, Mr. Gilliard, we're here to see if you can help us find out anything about the disappearance of a Robert T. Grantham. I believe you know him?"

"Oh, I'd say so. I've known Bob for better than twenty years now."

It turned out that even though Gilliard and Grantham had known each other for that extended period of time, the two did not socialize except on the golf course. Among the things he mentioned was that Grantham needed a golf cart in order to get around the course and required the assistance of a cane to get from the cart to the lie of his ball. Ever since his accident, he had needed one form of assistance or another.

"When was the last you saw or heard from Mr. Grantham?" Steve Davenport asked.

"The last time I saw him would have been at a tournament in Zolfo Springs. That would have been on a Saturday, just before he left to go to Las Vegas. The second? I think it was May second. A Saturday, anyway. I'm sure about that. It was a strictly amateur tournament. Hundred-dollar entry fee. That would have been the last time I saw the man. As for hearing from him, he called me when he was in Las Vegas.''

"Before that call, Mr. Gilliard, when you were in Zolfo Springs for the tournament, did Mr. Grantham say anything that you thought was unusual?''

"Not at all. He talked about his trip to Las Vegas. He was leaving in another couple days, of course, and seemed to be looking forward to it. I remember he said the last time he was there, that would have been about a month earlier, he won. I believe he mentioned the figure seventeen hundred dollars. He said he felt like his luck was still running and he wanted to take advantage of it at the tables.''

"Anything else?''

"No, not that I can think of in particular. Just, you know, golf talk. Joking around some. No real conversation, though.''

"And you say he called you after that, while he was in Las Vegas.''

"That's right. It would have been . . . I don't remember the date . . . it was in the evening. One evening, that's all.''

"That's all right. What did he talk about then?''

"Well, first we talked about his van, the one he uses in his business. It's an old Ford van, a sixty-eight, and I was doing some work on it for him. Then, while I thought we were still talking about the van, he pipes up that he's won forty-four hundred dollars so far, but he thinks somebody is cheating him.''

"Cheating?''

"That's what he said. But then you probably already know that what Bob says isn't always gospel. I mean, I wouldn't try to take his word to the bank, if you know what I mean.''

"Yes, we've heard that about him."

"Right, well, he says he thinks somebody is cheating him, even though he's won all that money, and he says he's afraid to go out of his room. That he's holed up in his room and won't go out. That's all he said about that, and I didn't ask him to tell me any more about it. I mean, with Bob . . ." Gilliard shrugged and shook his head.

Since Maurice Gilliard also had obvious misgivings about Grantham, Ray Velboom decided to take advantage of that fact and do a little fishing. "Just from what you know about our case, Mr. Gilliard, what do *you* think?"

Gilliard looked directly at him. "I suppose you already know about Bob taking off from time to time. Never mentioned to anyone that he was leaving and wouldn't be heard from for months at a time. Then one day he'd show up again like he hadn't ever been away. And never say a word about where he'd been or why.

"No, gents, I'm not convinced that Bob is dead. You'll have to show me his body before I'll believe it."

Velboom didn't say anything, but *some*body died in that Thunderbird.

Even his closest friends, though, believed it was not Lyin' Bob Grantham who was dead.

The FDLE agents closed their interview with Maurice Gilliard and thanked the Wauchula police chief, then drove back to Lakeland in pensive silence.

The very best that could be said about Bob Grantham was that the man was an enigma. But was he also a murderer? Or perhaps a murder victim? Velboom didn't feel the least bit closer to determining which of the two possibilities was true.

30

"Velboom."

"Yo."

"Call for you. Some guy named Kenneth Grantham."

Ray Velboom had been busy dictating notes for a typist to transcribe. He quickly put that chore aside and picked up the telephone. Kenneth, he recalled, was Robert Grantham's brother. "This is agent Velboom. Can I help you?"

Grantham introduced himself and said, "I understand you are looking into my brother's disappearance."

"That's right. How did you get my name?"

"Jacquelyn O'Hara told me you came out to see her. She's the one who told me he was missing to begin with."

"And are you calling to find out what we know about your brother's whereabouts?"

"Actually, no. Jacquelyn said you couldn't give out any information, and I appreciate that. What I'm calling for is to tell you about another call I got. From my aunt. Her name is Dorothy Booey. She lives in Auburndale."

"Yes?" Velboom pulled a notepad close to him and picked up a pen, ready to take down the information.

"She called just a couple minutes ago and said she

got a phone call from a woman who told her Bob's body has been found in a motel room in Wauchula with two bullets in him.''

"Mr. Grantham, you can be sure if a body was found, I would know about it. I'm afraid your aunt is the victim of a prank call. I don't know why people do things like that, but it happens. I'm sorry. I hope you'll call her right back and let her know it isn't true.''

"You're sure?''

"Positive." Velboom quickly added, "You know, Mr. Grantham, we want to talk with you about your brother, anyway. Why don't we set a time now while you're on the phone.''

"Tomorrow would be good for me.''

"First thing tomorrow morning? At the Winter Haven Police Department?''

"Fine.''

After disconnecting from Kenneth Grantham, Velboom called Detective William McNally, who had already been helpful in the case, and asked if the FDLE agents could use McNally's office for their interview with the missing man's brother. McNally was quick to agree.

The following morning Velboom and Davenport introduced themselves to Kenneth Grantham, who turned out to be reserved to the point of seeming curt.

He and Bob, he told them, were not close and never had been. "It's more than just the difference in our ages,'' Grantham said. He did not elaborate on just what the age differential was, but Velboom judged Kenneth to be ten or even fifteen years younger than he knew Robert to be. "It's mostly because Bob is a ... how should I put this? He's a bad egg, that's all. He just isn't a very good person.''

"How so?''

"Lots of ways,'' Kenneth said and proceeded to give a few examples. "And lately,'' he concluded, "there've been rumors about Bob being involved in some sort of drug deal and money laundering or transfer scheme between Las Vegas and Memphis, Tennessee. I didn't talk to him about that because I hadn't seen him in quite a while. And the truth is that I probably wouldn't have asked him about it if I did see him. There's no point in asking Bob anything because you can't depend on him telling you the truth, anyway. He's a con artist and always has been. If you want my opinion, Bob's disappearance now is more than likely his own doing. It would be just like him to set up something to look like he's missing or murdered or something, especially if he has something to hide from somebody."

"Then you think he may have faked his own disappearance?"

"Yes, sir, I do. And I'll tell you something else. If he is all right but in hiding, he's most likely either in Memphis or in Orlando. He has friends in both those places. I think he'd go to one of those cities or the other."

"Is there anything else you can tell us that you think might be helpful?"

"No, sir, nothing I can think of at the moment. I'll say one more thing, though. I don't approve of the way my brother conducts himself. But he is my brother, and I'm concerned about him. If you do learn anything, I'd appreciate it if you would let me know. I do care about him, you understand."

"We'll let you know if anything turns up," Velboom promised.

After telling Kenneth Grantham good-bye, the agents once again found themselves on the horns of a dilemma.

Once more there was the conflict of possibilities. Lyin' Bob Grantham once again came across as the sort who might easily feign his own abduction for purposes of his own. And yet he was also the sort who might well be involved in some underworld deal that could put his life at risk. His own brother believed he was involved in narcotics and/or money laundering. And Las Vegas was the city from which he called several different friends to tell them he was afraid to leave his hotel room because someone was after him.

Robert Grantham was turning out to be a most elusive character—in more ways than one.

31

"As soon as I got back into town, I checked in at work. The boss told me you stopped by a week or so ago. He said you were asking questions about Bob. So I called you right away."

Ray Velboom was back in Wauchula talking with truck driver, and close friend of Robert Grantham, Les Baker. Steve Davenport hadn't made the trip this time, deciding instead to remain in Lakeland and catch up on other work unrelated to the Grantham disappearance.

"I appreciate you contacting me so promptly," Velboom said.

"No problem."

"How long have you known Robert Grantham?"

"Oh, six or seven years. We met at the Little Cypress Golf Course here in Wauchula. We've been playing golf together ever since. He and I both love the game. He'd come down to Wauchula almost every weekend. Most often he'd stay at the Tropicana Motel and on Friday nights we'd get together with some of the guys and play a little poker. Then the next morning our golfing group would meet at Senterfits Restaurant for breakfast, then head on out to the course.''

''I understand you were supposed to go to Las Vegas with him?''

''Yeah. He asked me to go as his guest. He really had a good time when he was out there before, but he wanted company this trip. He offered to buy me a round-trip ticket and even give me a thousand dollars to gamble with. I took him up on it, but like you already know, I had to cancel out. Had to work. I had to take a load up north.''

''Your boss said you played with Grantham in a golf tournament the weekend before he left for Vegas.''

''We were supposed to play on that Saturday, but I was sick, so I didn't make it.''

''We've already spoken with Jacquelyn O'Hara. She told us that Mr. Grantham first wanted her to buy four plane tickets. Do you know who the other two people were that he was planning on taking on the trip with you?''

''Sure. He wanted to take a couple girls from here in town. Both waitresses at the Golden Corral restaurant. I know a girl named Jackie Brown was one of them. Then it turned out they couldn't—or maybe wouldn't, I'm not for sure about that—go either. I don't think Bob was too concerned about it when those two fell through because by then he was all hot and bothered about another girl, the daughter of one of the guys we play golf with, and he was after her to go with him when Jackie backed out. Bob was really stuck on this other girl.'' Baker laughed. ''But then that's the way Bob is, you know. He goes crazy over every girl he meets.''

''Do you know this other girl?''

''No, I've never met her. And really, I don't think Bob ever did actually take her out. I think he just wanted to awful bad. That's another thing about him, though. He gets crazy about these girls and starts to fantasize about them. I think half the time he really believes they're as crazy about him as he wants them to be.''

"Really?"

"Yeah. Like that last weekend before he left for Vegas. You were asking me about the tournament, right?''

"Uh huh.''

"Well, I hadn't seen Bob that day, and I wanted to see how his game went and, like, tell him good luck. I'd really been wanting to make that trip with him, you know. So I tried to call him. It took me, it must have been two, three hours before I could get through to him. After I figured he should be home, that is. And when I finally did get him, he bragged to me how he'd won his flight—maybe he really did, I don't know—and then he was saying how he'd met Maurice's daughter—that's our friend Maurice Gilliard, I mean—Bob was saying how he'd met Maurice's daughter Connie and did I know her. Well, I told him that I'd heard of her, of course, but that I didn't really know her. Then Bob got to telling me how they'd met at the golf course that day and she was just so crazy about him and how he'd— how should I put this—how him and her'd had sex together. And that she was going to meet him again later that night at some park and he was gonna get her again. He kept talking about her as 'my girl' this and 'my girl' that. But I can't say that I actually believed much of what he was telling me. I mean, Bob is an awful good friend. But even with his closest friends, he's kind of thrifty with the truth—if you know what I mean.''

Velboom smiled and acknowledged that he'd heard that already about Robert Grantham.

That was when Les Baker told Grantham that he would have to go to Las Vegas alone, Baker went on to explain. "There wasn't anything I could do about it except, you know, apologize. I didn't have a choice.''

"Did Grantham seem upset?"

"Disappointed, but I wouldn't say he was actually upset about it. He wasn't angry or anything like that. He did say he had something up his sleeve and maybe he could find a last-minute substitute. I don't know if he did or not. And then I wished him luck, in Vegas and with finding somebody else to go with him, too. That was the last time I've talked with him." Baker sighed and looked off into the distance.

Ray Velboom looked down at his notes. It seemed there were at least two more people he was going to have to interview: Jackie Brown, who worked at the Golden Corral, and Maurice Gilliard's daughter, Connie.

After thanking Les Baker for his help and seeing the man out of the borrowed office in the Wauchula police station, Velboom put in a call to Steve Davenport.

Velboom suggested they get together for lunch at the Golden Corral in Wauchula.

32

Velboom was waiting in the parking lot when Steve Davenport pulled into the Golden Corral. The restaurant proved to be one of those places that specializes in inexpensive steaks and an expansive salad bar. The two FDLE agents went through the line to order their meals, then found a table, where they waited to be served. While they waited they tried to decide which of the several waitresses would turn out to be Robert Grantham's sometime—or perhaps, imaginary—ladyfriend, Jackie Brown. They already knew enough about the missing man to realize it could prove to be virtually any woman in the place.

In fact, however, Steve Davenport chose the right woman, a freckled strawberry blond with a large bosom and even larger smile. After they finished their meal, and ascertained which of the waitresses was indeed Jackie Brown, they asked Miss Brown to sit and talk with them for a few minutes.

Jackie Brown first checked their identification and got permission from the restaurant manager, then joined the agents at their table. By then the lunch crowd has dissipated, and they had the immediate area to themselves.

Jackie Brown had already heard about Grantham's disappearance, so Velboom and Davenport got straight to business.

Yes, she did indeed know Grantham, she told them. She first met him when he came into the restaurant for lunch one day with some regulars. The men were talking about golf and apparently had just finished playing a round. One of the things she remembered in particular, she told the agents, was that Robert Grantham was far and away the loudest and most boisterous of the men at the table.

Among the things she remembered overhearing that time was Grantham's claim that he had just recently returned from Las Vegas. He was bragging about having won several thousand dollars while he was there.

"In this business you just naturally do overhear some stuff. You know? But this time, well, if I was going to bet I'd say that he knew perfectly good and well that I could hear when he was saying those things. In fact, I kind of got the idea he was saying them in particular when I was close by. I think he wanted me to hear about him winning."

Something else that would have been impossible to notice was Grantham's crude comments.

"When he was done eating and I asked him if he wanted anything else, he made some comment about my 'nice hot buns.' I said I was talking about dessert. He said so was he. All the guys at the table laughed, and of course I did too. You get a lot of stuff like that when you waitress, you know. Mostly guys don't mean anything. Most of them are just showing off for their buddies and would be scared to death if somebody really went and tried to take them up on some of the things they say when they're with their friends. Bob, I'm not so sure about. Anyway, this first time I saw him, all I said was that it wasn't on the menu. Then I went off to take care of my other tables."

"That wasn't the last time you saw Bob Grantham though, was it?"

"Oh no. He came in again the very next day."

And this time, she said, he was alone and not showing off for the benefit of his friends.

It was early for lunch and Grantham got coffee and a piece of cake. The lady at the counter noticed that he could not easily manage a cup and plate while handling his cane too, so she called for one of the waitresses to help him. The waitress she summoned, whether by chance or by request, was Jackie.

"He remembered my name from before. He didn't have to look at my name tag or anything. And he'd come back just to talk to me. I can tell you one thing I found out about him pretty quick, though."

"Yes?"

"You know how I said most guys when they talk big are doing it to show off for their buddies?"

"Yes."

"Not Bob. He's just a naturally obnoxious sort of person. All the time. He doesn't have to be with his friends for them to egg him on. He's like that anyway."

Steve Davenport looked away and tried to hide a smile behind his hand. It seemed to be true though. Their missing person was not the most sympathetic of potential victims.

"When I asked him how he was, he told me he was a lot better now that he could see my pretty face. And when I asked him where he wanted to sit, he said anywhere would be fine as long as he could have a clear view of me." She made a face. "Stuff like that. You know?"

Velboom nodded.

"I sat him at a table that wasn't one of mine to wait on, but that didn't stop him. He wanted me to sit with him. And really there wasn't anybody else in the place yet. We'd just opened for that day, you see. So it was like I didn't really have an excuse to not spend a minute or two with him.

"I hadn't any more than sat down when right off he asked me to go out with him that night."

She tried to stand up, intending to head for the kitchen, she said, but Grantham took her by the arm—not hard—just insistent. " 'Wait a minute, darlin'. Don't run off yet. I've got something I want to show you,' he said to me."

The man, a virtual stranger to her, reached into a pocket, she said, and pulled out a small black box. It was quite obviously a jewelry box.

"Go ahead. Open it."

Even so she hesitated.

"Aw, go on."

Against her better judgment she reached for the box.

"It isn't going to bite you."

She picked up the box and lifted the lid away. Inside, nesting on a puff of cotton, was a stunning diamond ring. Or at least what certainly looked like a diamond.

Surely, she thought, this odd man was not offering it to her. Something that beautiful . . .

"Well, aren't you going to try it on?" he prompted.

"Why?" she blurted. It was all she could get out.

Grantham chuckled.

"Because it's yours, that's why. Don't you like it?"

"It's beautiful. But why would you give it to me?"

"Because I like you."

"But we don't even know each other." Jackie was staring at the ring again. She couldn't help thinking about how it would look on her finger.

"I knew the first minute I saw you that I wanted to lay more than my eyes on you," Grantham said, then laughed so hard at his own joke that he probably didn't see Jackie cringe. When he stopped laughing he told her, "Seriously, I figured a good-looking girl like you wouldn't even give me the time of day. So I thought I'd sweeten the pot."

"What's the catch?" She put the ring on. She really couldn't help herself.

"Why, honey, there's no catch. Absolutely no strings attached. I just wanted to do something nice for you. There's no harm in that, is there?"

"I . . . guess not."

"Looks mighty nice on you, doesn't it?"

Jackie stretched out her hand so she could better admire the ring that seemed so perfect there on her finger. "I don't know what to say."

"You don't have to say anything at all, darlin', except that you'll go out with me tonight. And if you're worried about anything, why, we'll be double-dating with another couple. I've made plans with these people and I really need a date. Otherwise, I'd feel like the odd man out." He smiled.

She wasn't supposed to date the customers. But then, it was only a double date sort of thing. There would be other people along. It wasn't like she would be alone with the guy.

And the ring was awfully pretty.

Jackie nodded. "All right."

33

When Bob Grantham came by Jackie Brown's house that evening, the first thing she did was invite him inside, to meet her twelve-year-old son and her mother.

She was being polite, true. She was also making sure he knew she did not live alone. When they returned to the house later that evening, there would be others present. She wanted Grantham to know that and not think he could push his way inside and get grabby.

Grantham was cordial to Jackie's family. He told them a pleasant good evening and took Jackie outside to a white-top blue Ford Thunderbird, where another couple were in the backseat necking. Introductions were performed, more or less. The only name Jackie caught was Jerry.

Jackie sat silently in the car while they drove inland on State Road 64 to Avon Park, which, while a small town itself, is nonetheless considerably larger and more active than tiny Wauchula. The whole way there the couple in the back continued to smooch and giggle, while in the front seat Bob fiddled constantly with the radio dial in search of a station that would suit him. He didn't find one.

Eventually, to Jackie's great relief, they reached the Olympic Restaurant in Avon Park. Even there, though, things did not go well. The only person who seemed to be enjoying himself was Bob Grantham, who loudly, and tactlessly, built a conversation around the fact that Jerry recently had to borrow money from him and now could not pay it back. That hardly seemed the basis for an evening's entertainment, Jackie thought.

She found Grantham to be rude, boring, and frequently embarrassing. Several times she tried to change the subject. Grantham always insisted on bringing it back again to Jerry's financial difficulties and his own— Bob Grantham's, that is—ability to make money in large amounts.

When the dinner ended, Grantham insisted on paying for all of it. Jackie's impression was not that Bob was being generous, but that he was merely trying to underscore his own self-image of superiority.

No one said anything as they drove away—except, that is, Bob Grantham. He continued his discourse on how to make a substantial living.

Jackie was not surprised when Jerry and his date asked to be taken home immediately after dinner. It did not surprise her either to find that Grantham was entirely agreeable to that request. She felt sure the man was eager to be alone with her.

As soon as the other couple were out of the Thunderbird, though, Jackie "confided" to Bob that she had a simply awful headache and had it all through dinner. She told him she wanted to call it an evening too, even though it was still relatively early.

Grantham protested, but when Jackie insisted, he reluctantly took her back to her house.

When she paused still inside the car to thank him for the evening, Bob grabbed her and roughly started kissing her. She twisted out of his grasp and managed to get the car door open. Nearly falling in her eagerness to get outside the car safely, she slammed the door shut behind her and beat a hasty retreat to the safety of her home.

34

At age thirty, Jackie Brown had worked at the Golden Corral for the past year. The job was hard, but it was decent and dignified work, and Jackie thought herself lucky to be employed in a situation that allowed her to bring up a teenaged son without help.

Not that there was anything extra. Certainly not enough for her to buy extras like a beautiful diamond ring. The truth was that she really loved the ring that Bob Grantham gave her.

So it hurt her all the more when she lost it.

A few days after her less than wonderful date with Grantham, she was working in the kitchen at the Golden Corral. Pausing for a moment she held her hand out so she could admire the diamond. It was a habit she had come to quite thoroughly enjoy over the past few days. Except this time she was horrified to see that the setting was empty. The diamond was gone.

Jackie and her coworkers searched the entire kitchen feverishly, but the missing stone never turned up. Whether it went down the drain, fell into something, or whatever, they never knew. The diamond was gone for good.

Jackie was devastated. She was also uncertain what,

if anything, she should say to Grantham about it.

The man was calling her almost constantly, and Jackie felt guilty about losing such a valuable gift, even though he did not mention the ring to her when they spoke.

The best thing, she decided, would be to simply say nothing to him about the ring. And as for seeing him again, well, she had no intention of doing that anyway, even though he kept asking her to go out with him. Obviously, one rejection was not enough to discourage him.

A few days after her diamond disappeared, Jackie looked up from her work to see Bob Grantham standing there, staring at her figure.

And when he approached her practically the first thing out of her mouth, despite her resolve, was a blurted admission that she had lost the beautiful diamond he gave her.

She had expected anger. Instead he only shrugged, then smiled. "Is that the reason you been avoiding me, honey? Don't you worry about it, hear? Just give me the ring back and I'll have a new stone put in it. And this time I'll see they set it in nice an' tight. Okay?"

"You don't have to do that. You've already spent way too much on me as it is. I don't want you spending any more."

"Why not?" Grantham laughed. "I don't have anyone else to spend it on. And I've got plenty of it. Here, I'll show you." He took out his wallet and extracted a crisp fifty-dollar bill. "Here, take this."

"No, Bob. I can't do that."

"Sure you can. Go ahead."

She shook her head.

"Don't take it for yourself, honey. Take it for your son. You and him go buy him some new clothes or something. Go ahead." He grinned. "Besides, it'll make me happy if you take it."

Jackie accepted his rationalization, and the fifty. She slipped the nearly new bill into her apron pocket where she kept her tips and gave him the empty ring setting that she'd carried there ever since she lost the diamond.

Bob casually took the ring back and dropped it into his shirt pocket. Jackie never saw it again. If he had it repaired, she never knew about it, and never had nerve enough to ask.

Before she could say anything more Bob pointed to another waitress who was bending over to clear a nearby table. "Who's your friend?"

Jackie thought it a cheeky question with her standing right there beside him. Still, if there was anything you could say about Bob Grantham, it was that he was indeed damn well cheeky. In fact, that might be one of the nicest true things anyone could think to say about him. "Her name is Jerris," she told him.

"Who?"

Jackie spelled it for him.

"Jerris," he repeated. Then grunted and nodded to himself. "She's cute. See if she'll come over so I can say hi to her, would you, hon'?"

Against her better judgment, Jackie beckoned for Jerris to join them. She made short work of the introductions.

"Listen," Bob said, "I had some luck not too long ago in Las Vegas, and a friend and I are planning to go back there pretty soon. We thought it might be fun to bring along a couple pretty ladies to make things more interesting. I've already decided to take Jackie with me," which was news to Jackie, who was herself hearing it for the first time, "and when I saw you I thought you looked like you might enjoy a short vacation, too. What do you say, Jerris?"

Jerris looked at Jackie, who was just as startled by this question out of left field.

Before either girl could respond, Grantham picked up his cane and said, "Think it over, ladies. And don't worry about what it will cost. I'm picking up the bill for both of you. Travel, room, a little fun money to gamble with. It won't cost either one of you a cent.''

With that he made an unhurried exit, not bothering to look back to see what impression he may have left behind.

Silent until the man was outside, the two girls looked at each other. And, rolling their eyes, broke into laughter. The guy was crazy. Loony tunes. His idea was preposterous.

Or was it?

Before long it not only seemed a reasonable suggestion, it seemed a pretty darn good one. After all, they could just make sure they were together all the time. Every single moment. They wouldn't have to be alone with either one of the men.

When Bob called her that night, Jackie told him she and Jerris would go with him and his friend to Vegas.

"That pleased him a lot. I went out with him a couple more times after that, and he talked a lot about how much fun it was going to be in Las Vegas. But then Jerris backed out. She couldn't find anybody to stay with her kids for a whole weekend, so she couldn't go. He really got mad about that. He'd made plans and everything, I guess, and it really seemed to upset him when I said if Jerris wasn't going, then I wouldn't feel right about going off for a weekend with two men, so I didn't want to go either. He blew up and said he didn't want to see me again if I backed out of my promise to go off with him. It really surprised me when he reacted like that. I never talked to him again after that night.''

"He didn't call you from Las Vegas?'' Velboom asked.

"No, I never spoke to him again.''

"What about Jerry?''

"She doesn't work here anymore.''

"No, not Jerris. Jerry. The man who was along on that double date. From what you said, he might have had reason to be mad at Robert Grantham.''

"Oh, like about the money he owed and how Bob talked about him?" Jackie shrugged. "I don't recall if I ever heard his last name. To tell you the truth, I can't even remember what town we were in when Bob dropped him and his girl off that night. I wasn't exactly having the best time and wasn't paying much attention. I'm sorry."

Velboom glanced down at his notes. They had gotten more from Jackie Brown than he had expected, if less than he hoped for.

And if they could find this Jerry, well, they'd talk to him. Maybe some other friend of Robert Grantham would be able to put a last name to Jerry—who might, just might, have a strong enough reason to cause bodily harm to the overbearing Mr. Grantham.

"Thanks for your help, Miss Brown. Thank you very much."

35

Steve Davenport picked up the phone in the Lakeland FDLE office after just one ring.

"Agent Davenport?"

"Yes, that's right."

"This is Rudy Benton. I talked to you just a couple days ago at the Wauchula police station."

"I remember you, Mr. Benton. What can I do for you?"

"You said I should call if I found out anything more you might be interested in."

"Yes, of course."

"Well, I got a call from Bob's ex-wife. You know her, I think. Jacquelyn O'Hara? And she said something that I thought was kind of strange."

"Yes?"

"She said that if Bob is dead that she will end up inheriting everything he owns. I don't know why she thinks she'd have a claim on his estate, but she plans on taking over his property. She's already running the business, she said. She's lined up a roofing job at a phosphate mine that she told me she'll make sixteen thousand dollars off of."

"That's very interesting, Mr. Benton," Davenport said, thinking otherwise. "Did she say anything else?"

"No, that's it."

"Well, thank you for letting us know, Mr. Benton. I appreciate your call." That much was the truth. Rich nuggets can be found in the strangest of streams.

It occurred to Davenport that there was only silence at the other end of the line. Rudy Benton seemed reluctant to say good-bye. And perhaps there was a reason for that.

"Mr. Benton?"

Benton cleared his throat. "I'm, uh, sorry. But there's something else. I'm just having a hard time deciding whether or not it's important. If it isn't, see, I'd rather not go into it. You see, Maurice Gilliard is a real good friend of mine, and I'd hate to say or do anything that would upset him. But I have this information. Maybe it's something you should know. I just can't be sure."

"You know, Mr. Benton, Maurice Gilliard is a good friend of Robert Grantham's too. I'm sure he would want all of us to do everything we can to find out if Grantham is all right. And if your information isn't important, it stops right here and no harm will be done."

"I expect that's true." Benton hesitated a few seconds longer, then said, "It's about Maurice's daughter. Connie Gilliard, her name is. Connie Gilliard Beasley, actually. That was her married name, though she's been divorced for three or four months. She and her two kids are living with her parents for the time being."

"Yes?" Davenport pulled a notepad in front of him and picked up a pen. Connie Gilliard's name had come up before. He had to think for a moment to recall who had mentioned her. The name had been in the report Ray Velboom made on his conversation with Les Baker. The trucker had said this Connie was Robert Grantham's passionate love interest just before he left for Las Vegas. "What about her, Mr. Benton?" asked Davenport.

"Maybe nothing. But I was thinking back to a talk I had with her just before Bob vanished. I don't know if it means anything, of course. But I thought you ought to know about it. Just in case. You know?"

"Tell me about it, please."

"Hello."

"Rudy? This is Connie Beasley, Rudy. Maurice Gilliard's daughter?"

"I remember you, Connie. How are you?"

"Fine."

"The kids?"

"We're all just fine, thanks. You, uh, are you going to be at the golf tournament that's coming up?"

"Yes. Your dad is too."

"I know. Mama and I are meeting him there for the picnic after." There was a rather long pause.

"So what's up, Connie?" Getting a call from Maurice's daughter was not exactly a common occurrence. Rudy knew there had to be a good reason behind it.

"Look, I'm not real sure how to put this. But you play golf with Bob Grantham, don't you?"

"Yes, we play pretty often. He's supposed to be at that tournament too, you know."

"Yes, I do know. Look, uh, Rudy, you know Grantham pretty well, don't you?"

"I'd say that I do, Connie."

"I wouldn't want you to say anything about this to daddy, what I'm going to tell you."

"All right."

"But Bob has been hitting on me pretty hard. He seems real taken with me."

Rudy laughed. "That sounds like Bob, all right. You're a pretty girl, Connie. Bob never has been able to resist a pretty girl. Would you like me to tell him to back off?"

Again there was a long silence. "That isn't exactly what I wanted to know, Rudy."

"No?"

"The thing is . . . promise you won't tell daddy about this?"

"All right. I promise."

"The thing is, Rudy, Bob has been saying he'd give me thirty thousand dollars if I'll sleep with him."

"Yes?"

"So what I was wondering . . . I mean you know him and everything . . . what I was wondering is . . . does Bob really have that kind of money?"

Rudy chuckled silently to himself. It was not lost on him that she'd asked if Bob had the money. Not if she should share the sheets with him if the money really was available. And wasn't that interesting about Maurice's little girl. Still, it was her business, not his. And she hadn't exactly asked for his advice, so there was no sense in him trying to give her any.

"Let me answer you this way, Connie. I'd say what you ought to do is get a look at the money first. Then do what you think is best."

"Yeah, I suppose so."

"Better yet, Connie, maybe what you ought to do is get half the money up front. And then not go through with the rest of it."

"You know, that's a funny thing, Rudy. You're the second person who's told me that same thing." She laughed and soon disconnected, leaving Rudy Benton wondering if he'd said the right thing. After all, Bob was his friend, but then so was Maurice. He shrugged and tried to put the conversation out of mind.

"And did she go through with it?" Steve Davenport asked.

"Oh, I doubt it. Although I'll tell you this. I like Connie okay and I like her dad an awful lot. But I think if somebody laid the money down in front of her, Connie would do whatever it took to get that cash in her purse. If you know what I mean."

"I do, Mr. Benton. And thank you very much for the information."

"Sure."

"My partner and I will want to talk to Connie, I suppose. Do you know where we can find her?"

"She's living with her folks like I told you, but she's working at the Buick dealership in Bartow. You know it?"

"I forget the name, but it's on State Road 60 on the bypass, right?"

"That's the place. It's called Remsgar Buick."

"All right, Mr. Benton. Thank you very much."

This time Benton was willing to hang up without any foot-dragging.

Davenport immediately put a call through to Ray Velboom. Connie Gilliard Beasley definitely had to be put on the list of persons to interview.

36

It was mid-afternoon of the following day before FDLE special agents Ray Velboom and Steve Davenport could make the short drive south from Lakeland to Bartow. Remsgar Buick was located on the north side of town close to the Lakeland-Bartow highway.

Connie Beasley proved to be an extremely attractive young woman in her mid-twenties. It took no leap of the imagination to see why a man with Robert Grantham's near legendary interests, and persistence, would want to chase her. It was another question to think about why she might consider responding. Until, that is, Davenport remembered there were roughly thirty thousand good reasons for her to weigh in the equation.

One thing both agents noticed: Either Connie Beasley expected to be questioned about Grantham or she hid her surprise awfully well when Velboom and Davenport displayed their identification and introduced themselves to her. Connie very matter-of-factly led the men to one of the glass-walled sales cubicles lining the display room floor and invited them to make themselves comfortable.

A moment later she volunteered the information that she had been expecting them or at least expecting someone to talk with her. "I heard about Bob disappearing, you know. And it isn't any secret that I knew him. He was a friend of my father's for a long time, you know.''

"We appreciate your cooperation, Mrs. Beasley."

"Miss, please. Or just Connie. But I'm not Mrs. Beasley anymore."

"Yes, uh, whatever you prefer."

"Connie would be just fine, thank you.'' She smiled and leaned back, crossing her legs and clasping her hands over her knee. She seemed quite comfortable behind the large, uncluttered sales desk that held a calendar, a blotter, a telephone, and not much else.

"Let's start from the top then," Velboom suggested. "First, and just for the record, where do you live?"

"I live with my parents in Wauchula."

"Isn't that a pretty long drive from here?'' Having made the trip himself all too frequently in recent days, Velboom knew good and well the trip normally took an hour or so.

"It gets old making that drive every day. But then what would I do in Wauchula? Work for my dad? He owns a used car place there, and I suppose I could work for him if I had to. But really. Living with your parents at my age is one thing. Working with them too, that'd be just too, too much."

"I can understand that,'' Velboom said pleasantly. "How long have you been with Remsgar?''

"Six months. Something around there, anyhow."

"And how long have you known Robert Grantham?''

"A couple months. Something like that. He and my father have known each other for a long time, but I only met him for the first time in April, I think it was. It was a Saturday about the middle of the month and they'd just finished a golf game. . . .''

Finished with their play fairly early, the customary group of golfers headed for their cars, Bob Grantham setting the pace with his cane and the others trailing slowly along with him.

"Are you in a hurry to get home, Bob?" Maurice Gilliard asked.

"Nope. In fact I'm not going home just yet. I want to stop over at the Golden Corral to see my girl Jackie. Maybe I'll stay over tonight so her and me can have a nice time."

"Could you give me a ride home on your way?" Gilliard asked. "It isn't far."

"Sure. You can see how this 'Bird of mine rides. Like floating on a cloud, I tell you."

Grantham loaded his golf bag into the trunk of the Thunderbird while Maurice stuffed his behind the front seat so that he could get it out without Bob having to get out of the car again and open the trunk lid. They said good-bye to the rest of the bunch, and Grantham drove to Maurice's home on the east side of Wauchula.

The house was a nice enough split-level, if a trifle sparse when it came to landscaping. The grass was brown from too little watering, and the only planting in the yard was a none too healthy looking little oak that was struggling to establish itself.

Beside the oak were a pair of small children playing in the grass and a very attractive blond woman wearing shorts and a sleeveless blouse. When Grantham pulled into the driveway, Maurice reached across to the steering wheel and honked the horn. The young woman waved, said something to the children, and she came trotting over to the car.

"Who's that?" Grantham asked in a voice normally reserved for the interior of churches, during funeral services, or at other particularly sacred moments.

"That's my daughter," Maurice said proudly.

Grantham let out a low whistle. "You know, Maurice, you and I have been playing together for years, but I never once knew you had such a gorgeous daughter."

Maurice laughed and made the introductions.

Obviously reacting to Connie's last name, Grantham bluntly asked, "Are you married?"

"No, divorced."

"Really. What do you do for a living, honey?"

She told him.

"That's interesting. Y'know, Connie, I've been thinking about trading my Thunderbird here for something newer. Maybe I should stop by Remsgar and, um, check out what you have, huh?"

"Sure. Come on by any time. Maybe we'll have what you want."

"I just bet you do, Connie. I just bet you do." Grantham chuckled.

Two days later, first thing in the morning, Connie was paged by the showroom speaker. "Ms. Beasley, line two. Ms. Beasley."

She went to the nearest desk and picked up the telephone. "This is Connie, how can I help you?"

"Remember me?"

It was a man's voice. She did not recognize it. "No, I'm sorry, I don't."

"You have no idea?"

"No," she said, deliberately sharp this time.

"Don't you remember meeting me? I'm a good friend of your father's."

She did remember him then. He had said something about maybe wanting a car. But she could not recall his name. That was something she needed to work on. Really successful salespeople are most often the ones who develop a knack for remembering, and liberally using, their customers' names. She decided to remain silent rather than admit she could not remember the man's name.

"This is Bob Grantham, honey."

"Of course I remember you now, Mr. Grantham."

"Bob. Please call me Bob."

"All right, Bob. What can I do for you?"

Bob Grantham with his beloved dogs
(Courtesy of Jacquelyn O'Hara)

Steve Davenport *(left)* and Ray Velboom

(Courtesy of the author)

Jacquelyn O'Hara

(Courtesy of the author)

The interior of Bob Grantham's Thunderbird. A newspaper and Redman box were placed on the seat in an effort to hide the bloodstains.

(Courtesy of Florida Department of Law Enforcement)

The contents of the Thunderbird's trunk. Note the absence of a wheelchair.

(Courtesy of Florida Department of Law Enforcement)

Robin Boney

(Courtesy of the author)

John Skye

(Courtesy of the author)

A diving team from the Hillsborough Sheriff's Department looks for the murder weapon.

(Courtesy of Hillsborough County Sheriff's Office)

"Look, I drove by Remsgar yesterday. There was a blue Trans-Am sitting out front. How much do you want for that car?"

"I can't tell you that over the telephone, Bob. You should come in and look at the car first. Then we can take a look at your trade-in and discuss the numbers."

"Come on, Connie. I'm your dad's buddy. You can tell me."

"I'm sorry, Bob, but I really can't. But if you come in, our business manager will sit down with you and talk price. That's our policy here."

"Connie, you sound like you aren't interested in making a commission on this deal."

"That isn't it at all, Bob. I'm just trying to follow the rules."

"Now that's good, honey, because the way I hear it, you could use the money. In fact, I think you ought to get a better break."

"Pardon me?"

"I've been asking around about you, Connie. You're twenty-five years old and living with your parents. And you have those two children to take care of. That's no way to live, honey. I'd sure like to see you do better than that. In fact, I think you can do better. And I'd be willing to help you do it."

Connie shivered. What was this guy doing checking up on her like that, finding out stuff about her private life? And what was this about him helping her to do better? This Bob guy seemed awfully strange and certainly plenty forward. "Mr. Grantham, why are you so . . . interested in my welfare?"

"Hey, you're my buddy's daughter, aren't you? And besides, Connie, you're a real looker."

"Is that what this is about? Look, Mr. Grantham, I have to go now. Nice talking to you."

"Wait a minute, Connie. How would you like thirty thousand dollars?"

"Thirty . . . what?"

"I'm serious, Connie. I'll give you thirty thousand. That should help you and the kids establish yourselves."

"And what would I have to do to earn this thirty thousand dollars of yours, Mr. Grantham?"

"You know good and well what you'd have to do, Connie. You'd have to be my lover."

"Just like that?"

"Sure. Why not?"

"Are you nuts?"

He laughed. "Not at all. Look, Connie, you didn't notice it the other day because I never got out of the car. But I have to walk with canes or be in a wheelchair all the time. That's because of an accident I had. The thing is, I'm about to reach a settlement for my claim, and I'm going to come into some serious money. The thirty thousand for you and your kids will be pocket change compared with that. I can afford it easy. And I can't think of a better way to spend it than on you. I saw that first thing when I got a look at you, Connie. You're the real stuff."

"Mr. Grantham, you're sick." She hung up on him.

Moments later she was paged again. "I think we got cut off," Bob Grantham's voice said through the telephone.

"I'd rather you didn't call here any more."

"You haven't answered my question, Connie."

"Yes, I have. I'm not going to sleep with you. Not for any amount of money."

He laughed again, not at all discouraged by her initial rejection.

"I'm not a whore, Mr. Grantham, and I'm not going to sleep with you. And that's final." She slammed the receiver down again.

He called back again, of course. She had thought he would. He called back several times over the course of the next few days. Eventually she asked her father what to do about it and was told not to worry about it, that Bob was brassy and sometimes foolish but harmless.

He approached her again in person at the picnic following a golf tournament in Zolfo Springs, but there her mother ran interference for her and tried to make sure Connie never had to be alone with Grantham. Her mother did not like Grantham and often referred to him as "that son of a bitch."

At the last minute, Grantham called her at work once more and asked her to go with him to Las Vegas. She could get an idea of what it would be like to have money—and some fun. Again she hung up on him.

Later he called her several times from Las Vegas to brag about how much money he was winning and to suggest that they spend some of it when he got back home.

"He's a creepy one," Connie said, making a face.

There was no mention in Connie's yarn, Ray Velboom noted, about the fact that she considered Grantham's offer seriously enough to seek Rudy Benton's counsel about Robert Grantham's ability to pay.

But then that was hardly unusual. People tend to be strict when it comes to the ethical standards they demand in others, but somewhat more understanding of their own occasional wavering.

"And you have no idea where Grantham is now?"

"No. I heard from him when he was in Las Vegas. At least that's where he said he was calling from. You couldn't prove it by me. I haven't heard from him since."

Steve Davenport sighed and shifted position in his chair. The chair was padded but proved to be considerably less comfortable than its appearance suggested.

"By the way, you probably heard the rumor about Bob and me having some sort of relationship," Connie casually volunteered.

''No, actually we haven't,'' Davenport told her.

''People have been talking. But let me tell you right now, any relationship that man ever had with me existed only in his own mind. I think he told some of his buddies that he was sleeping with me, but it isn't true. What I really believe is that Les Baker and Rudy Benton put him up to asking me out, kind of egging him on to make fun of both him and me, and that he made up these stories about me to save face with his friends. I've heard there is a rumor that claims I met him one night at Pioneer Park, but there's no way I would have had anything to do with somebody like him. The man is disgusting.''

''Yes, well, we haven't come across any rumors like that, but don't worry. We're much more interested in facts than in rumors.'' Ray Velboom smiled and was about to thank her for her time, but Connie was not done talking.

With neither preamble nor apparent purpose she launched into a long and not particularly interesting account having to do with a traffic ticket she got not long before. Something about driving her boyfriend's car and losing control. But she wasn't drunk, the pavement was wet, and that was why the car spun around like it did. And then this cop in Tampa seeing the whole thing and writing her a ticket, and then she was in the hospital the day she was supposed to appear in court, and then she got this notice thing in the mail and had to turn herself in to the sheriff in Brandon, and then she was treated so awfully bad in jail, put in there with prostitutes and all sorts of undesirables and the matron was rough and rude and she had *bruises*, right there on her arm they could see for themselves bruises. . . .

Velboom stifled a yawn and tuned her out, sitting with a polite if uninterested expression until she ran out of steam. It happened sometimes, people wanting someone, anyone, to complain to because authority, the system, the world, was not treating them fairly.

Davenport and Velboom sat through the recitation with all the aplomb of bored professionalism, then thanked Connie for her help and made their escape before she could think of something else she wanted to tell them.

37

The first round of interviews—talking with the people who were the most likely to have some knowledge of the case—was complete. Now it was time for Velboom and Davenport to sit down with their superiors and fill them in on what progress, if any, they'd made on the case so far.

After all, it was still conjecture to assume that there had been a death in that abandoned Ford Thunderbird. They were still a long way from proving even that, much less who the presumed murder victim may have been.

Ray Velboom and Steve Davenport were in the position of the hunter who found tracks in the snow. No matter how fresh those tracks were, they made a mighty thin soup.

And that was the essence of what they would be able to report when they sat down to meet with Bureau Chief Ed Williams and with Velboom's immediate supervisor, E.J. Picolo.

They met in the conference room at the Tampa office and, fortified with some freshly brewed coffee, prepared to tell what they knew, or, more to the point, what they didn't.

After a little easy banter, Ed Williams asked how the investigation was going. Both Velboom and Davenport cringed.

"That bad?"

"Well we've been able to gather some information," Velboom began, "but—"

"None of it meshes," Davenport finished for his partner.

"The more we learn, the more confusing this one becomes," Velboom said.

"Tell us about it," Picolo suggested.

Davenport motioned for Velboom to proceed, and the special agent began at the beginning with Jacquelyn O'Hara and Robin Boney.

"The thing is, we can't even decide if Robert Grantham is a killer or a victim. We talk to one person and lean one way. The next person we interview turns it the other way."

While Williams and Picolo let their coffee get cold as they concentrated on what the two field agents were telling them, Velboom and Davenport together laid out what they knew.

Grantham had a fairly extensive criminal history, including a pattern of vanishing at times in the past without telling anyone where he was going or what he was up to. The man had worked at both the Orlando and Tampa airports in the past. And, perhaps most telling of all, he may well have been involved in the suspicious death of a man in Louisiana.

Grantham even switched identities with the dead man in that case in an effort, or so he explained, to throw off certain unnamed parties who were allegedly pursuing him. He wanted them, whoever they were, to think he was the dead man and, therefore, leave him alone.

"Is there anything to indicate he has done the same thing again?" Picolo asked.

There was no concrete evidence to support that theory. But on the other hand, several people who knew Grantham—not the man's enemies but his own associates and close friends—believed it was entirely possible that Grantham once again manufactured his own disappearance.

Williams leaned back in his chair and grimaced—at once puzzled and dissatisfied.

"And there is also the wheelchair," Velboom added.

"I don't remember seeing anything in the reports about a wheelchair," Picolo said.

"Exactly," Velboom agreed.

"Would you mind explaining?"

"There is no wheelchair. You know Grantham was injured a while back. He can only get around by way of a wheelchair or cane. Apparently he used the cane most of the time and kept the wheelchair in the trunk of the Thunderbird. Except we haven't come across the wheelchair. The cane was in the car, but there was no wheelchair. And nothing was found at the airport. The wheelchair is missing."

Picolo and Williams had no trouble reaching the inevitable conclusion suggested by Velboom's statement. "So you feel the missing wheelchair gives credence to the theory that Grantham is the murderer, since he would need either the chair or his cane to get away from the scene," Williams said.

Velboom nodded.

Picolo leaned forward. "Let me ask you this. Besides the so-called drug dealers from Louisiana who might still be after him, did Grantham have any other reason for disappearing?"

"It's possible. Tenuous—although what isn't in this case—but possible. His own brother suggested he might have been involved in drugs and money-laundering. In fact, those rumors say the money laundering scheme may have been in Vegas and possibly Tennessee. And we know Grantham visited Las Vegas twice in the few months before he vanished. He was also a hard-core gambler and womanizer. Between the two of those, he could probably work up enough fresh trouble to have to drop out of sight for awhile''—Velboom paused—''even to make it look like he'd been murdered so someone would stop looking for him. Don't forget, he called several different people back here in Florida and told them he was hiding in his room and was afraid to go out. Those claims could have been a set-up to support his disappearance, or they could have been true and a reason for him to go into hiding.''

After letting this sink in, Davenport and Velboom went on to show the flip side of the coin. Davenport took the lead in presenting it. ''There is also,'' he said, ''the hypothesis we originally went with. And that one has Robert Grantham as the victim.''

''Go ahead,'' Williams said.

''When he was in Vegas making all those phone calls we already mentioned,'' Davenport said, ''he told his friends more than just that he was scared. He also said he was winning. That he had a large amount of cash in his pockets. And whether he won at the casinos on that trip or not, we know that it was his habit to carry a wad. Worse, he liked to flash it. He liked showing off, especially to the ladies. And then again, we have those calls saying he was afraid to leave his room, that someone was after him. Well, maybe someone was. It's like the old saw about the nut case. Just because a guy is paranoid, it doesn't mean there isn't somebody after him.''

''You think somebody followed him back to Florida and killed him for his money?'' Picolo asked.

''It's certainly possible,'' Velboom said. ''But there are other suspects closer to home.''

Between them Velboom and Davenport recounted at

least some of the possibilities. There was Tressa Brantley's girlfriend, who once openly talked about how easy a target Grantham would be if someone wanted a robbery victim. There was Bill (last name unknown), who was angry with Grantham for taking photos of Bill's girlfriend in the nude. And there was Jerry, whose last name was also as yet unknown, who owed Grantham money and who was humiliated by Grantham during the double date with Jackie Brown.

"We also need to look closer at his niece. After all, she had her sentencing rescheduled for a time, which turned out to be remarkably convenient once her uncle disappeared."

"You're long on possibilities but a little short on certainties, aren't you?" Picolo observed.

"Tell us about it."

"One thing I notice you haven't mentioned is the lab work on the car. What about the blood type match with Grantham? Sure there are millions of guys in this country with Type A, so a match wouldn't prove anything about the victim. But if Grantham is listed as something other than A. . . ." It was not necessary to finish the sentence. They all knew that would mean he would be unequivocally eliminated as the person murdered in the vehicle.

Davenport reluctantly admitted that so far they had not been able to find any record, anywhere, to show Robert Grantham's blood type.

"You would think the hospital would have it. He went through several operations there after his accident. But for some reason, his record doesn't list his blood type. It sounds crazy, but it's true. We're still looking."

"Something else occurs to me," Williams said. "We can't prove that Grantham is the victim, but I haven't heard the name of any *other* person who might logically be the victim from that car."

"No, sir."

"So the only pursuable theory we have at this point

involves Grantham as the victim and parties unknown
as the perpetrator or perpetrators.''

"Yes, sir.''

"Concentrate on that then, at least for the time being.
Take a closer look at everyone who could conceivably
be responsible if it does turn out that Grantham is the
guy who died in that automobile.''

"Yes, sir.''

That was an instruction that they would, in fact, not
follow. But none of them could know that at the time.

38

Several hours after the briefing with Williams and Picolo, Ray Velboom was putting together a list of things
they needed to do when the duty officer interrupted him.

"Phone call, Ray. Woman says her name is Robin
Boney.''

There were calls Velboom would rather take than requests from family members for information. He understood full well how concerned relatives could be. But it
was never in the best interests of an investigation to give
out information on the progress of a case. And anyway,
it was downright embarrassing to realize, whether he
admitted it to the relatives or not, that in truth they were
making virtually no progress here.

This time, however, the family member was calling
not to inquire about progress, but to offer information.

"Do you remember when we talked about my uncle's wheelchair?"

"Of course. That is something that has been really puzzling us." He did not elaborate on the significance of the missing chair. That would have been cruel, as good as accusing the woman's uncle of being a murderer, and stupid as well, since it could very likely silence a potential witness.

"Jackie and I have been trying to keep things going until Uncle Bob gets home, you know. And, anyway, a bill came in that I thought you ought to know about."

"Yes?"

"It's from State Oxygen Services. It seems he has been renting his wheelchair from them, and for some reason he turned it back to them before he left for Las Vegas. He never said anything about getting a new one or anything like that. But anyway, the wheelchair is accounted for now. I thought you'd want to know."

Velboom frowned. But of course the information was more important than Robin Boney likely knew. It shot down their theory that Grantham was the killer and made it much more likely that he was the victim—just as Ed Williams had told them to pursue just those few short hours ago.

"Thank you very much," Velboom said, trying to keep his voice neutral. "Listen, while we're on the phone, how is your daughter? She was supposed to have that surgery by now, wasn't she?" Boney had mentioned her daughter's upcoming operation at their first meeting.

The child was just fine thank you, Boney told him. She was recuperating now and doing very well.

"I don't suppose your uncle showed up for the surgery like you thought he would."

"No. I really looked for him, too. I really thought he'd make it."

"I'm sorry, Robin. And if you don't mind me asking, how did your court hearing go?"

Taken momentarily aback by the direct question, Boney hesitated, then gave the agent information that he could easily get for himself, anyway. She was placed on two years community control, meaning she would be under the close and direct supervision of a probation officer for that period. It amounted to virtual house arrest since she would have permission to travel only to work, to the grocery, and to other events only by special permission of the probationary officer. It would be restrictive, but not nearly so much as a prison term would have been. She seemed to accept the sentence with equanimity, including a condition that she pay restitution of $1,957.92 to the NCNB bank.

"You know, the reason I asked my lawyer to delay the hearing date was so I could be with my little girl during her surgery. I was really afraid I was going to have to go to jail. Now it turns out I didn't have to worry about that, but I sure didn't know it at the time."

"No, of course you couldn't," Velboom told her while another of their many theories withered. So much for Robin Boney's continuance and potential reason for shunting her uncle aside. "Thank you for calling, Robin. And I'm awfully glad your daughter is okay now."

After disconnecting, he went back to his list of things yet to do, but there was definitely something that was nagging at him. Something in the files? Something in the information they had developed? He wasn't sure.

The FDLE office was busy at the moment, and the distractions were many. After a little while longer Velboom gathered up his case file and carried it home so that he could read through it again undisturbed.

Settling down in his kitchen with the reports and interview records scattered across his kitchen table, he went through each document over and over again.

And found . . . nothing.

Eventually he gave up and went to bed. Even then he

could not lay aside the thought that there was something out of place. He lay long into the night, wide awake and staring toward a darkened ceiling while he tried to make the missing connection.

39

"I don't know who you are or what you want, but this better not be a wrong number."

"It's Ray, Steve."

Davenport groaned. "Do you have any idea what time it is?"

"No, do you?"

Davenport cursed some but did not get around to answering. The question must surely be rhetorical.

"Look, Steve, put some clothes on and meet me at the Tampa office, will you?"

"I hope you have an awfully good reason for this."

"To tell you the truth, no. But I need your help. There is something that's bothering me, and I hope between the two of us we can figure out what it is."

Davenport sighed. "It will take me about an hour to dress and get over there."

"I'll already be there."

And so he was. Davenport and Velboom went over every word, every statement, every bit of evidence the two of them had collected about the disappearance of Robert Grantham.

They were still at it when the other agents began trickling in for the start of the day.

When they looked at the interview report with Rudy Benton, Velboom paid special attention. Something had been bothering him then, too, but he hadn't ever been able to figure out what it would have been.

"Benton was the last person to hear from Grantham," Davenport reminded his partner. "Grantham called him from the Orlando airport right after he got back from Vegas. Told Benton he'd won a lot of money and that he was going to pick up his luggage. They made plans to play golf that weekend."

Velboom sat bolt upright, his fatigue falling away and a broad grin coming over his face.

"What have you got?" Davenport asked, the excitement contagious even before he learned what was causing it.

"Steve, I've got it. What time did Grantham get into Orlando on the seventh?"

Davenport fingered through the papers to locate the one he wanted. "The flight touched down on time at four-thirty that afternoon."

"And what time did Grantham call Rudy Benton?"

Davenport whistled. "About nine o'clock that night."

"So if he arrived in Orlando in the afternoon, what was he doing still in the airport at nine that night?"

"Seems kind of unlikely, doesn't it."

"You know what I'd like to do?"

"Same thing I would. We want a look at Grantham's phone bill."

"Here's hoping he charged the call to his home number or a credit card, whenever he made it and from wherever."

Davenport stood. "I'm going to go by Grantham's house and see if the bill is there. You said Robin Boney and the ex are keeping the business going, right?"

"Cross your fingers, Steve."

"Aw, I can do better than that." With a grin Davenport was gone.

Velboom rubbed some of the grittiness from his burning eyes and thought he would go treat himself to a shower and a change of clothes while Davenport was chasing after the telephone bill.

And if nothing else, that nagging, niggling sensation was gone. At least he'd found the discrepancy that had been sending warning signals through his subconscious.

40

It was lunchtime when Steve Davenport returned with the telephone bill sent to Bob Duke, that being the name Grantham had used when listing his telephone and also presumably the name of the dead man found long ago in a Louisiana motel room.

The agents took the bill with them to a nearby Cuban restaurant and pored over it while they ate.

Several calls, they noticed, had been placed to a number in Bartow.

"Wait here." Steve Davenport took the bill with him and dialed the Bartow number, charging the call to the Florida Department of Law Enforcement. He was smiling when he returned to the table.

"Remsgar Buick," he said as he resumed his chair.

"The calls he made to Connie Beasley from Las Vegas."

"Right."

"This last call on the list . . ."

"Just a second. Let me look through this file and . . . here we go." Again Davenport smiled. "That's Rudy Benton's number."

The call to Benton, which Grantham told his friend was made from the Orlando airport while he was waiting for his luggage, was logged at 9:14 P.M. on May 7, 1987.

"His plane had been on the ground nearly five hours by that time," Velboom observed.

"Real slow luggage handlers, huh?"

"It doesn't say where the call was placed from."

"This bill doesn't. But somebody at GenTel will have that on file. Count on it."

"Let's ask them to flesh out the entire bill. Not just who was called but where each call originated."

Davenport nodded. This time it was Ray Velboom who excused himself and went to the pay phone. He called General Telephone's security department and identified himself as an FDLE agent, then explained what was needed: an analysis of each call billed to Bob Duke during the past month.

It would take, he was told, most of the afternoon for the information to be pulled together.

Velboom and Davenport finished their lunch, and then fidgeted through an afternoon of routine paper shuffling while they tried not to think about the possibility that the telephone bill could provide the revelation they needed.

It was nearly five o'clock when General Telephone had the information ready.

Slowly, item by dull item, the GenTel security man went through the bill, explaining each code and set of numbers. Velboom listened patiently until they reached the final entry, the last call Robert Grantham made on his credit card.

That call was placed at exactly 9:14 P.M. to Rudy Benton's number in Zolfo Springs, Florida. The call was charged to Bob Duke's General Telephone Company credit card. No revelations there by any means. Then Velboom asked what number the call was made from.

"The call was made from area code eight-one-three. . . . ''

Velboom didn't even hear the last seven digits that first time around.

Eight-one-three is the area code for Tampa and south-western Florida including Winter Haven and Lakeland. Orlando was in a completely different area code.

Grantham's last call could not have come from the Orlando airport like he told Rudy Benton.

But why would he lie about as simple a thing as that? And if not from Orlando, then where had he been calling from?

"Excuse me, but could you run that last number for me, the one from the eight-one-three area. I need to know whose number it is."

"Sure. It'll take maybe another hour or so."

"I'll be here. Believe me, I'll be here waiting."

Less than an hour later GenTel security was back on the line. The telephone from which Robert Grantham placed his call was listed to a Richard H. Anderson of 7523-C Pitch Pine Circle—in Tampa.

"Tampa?" Davenport asked.

"That's what the man said. Right here in Tampa."

Where, of course, the bloody and abandoned car was located some days later.

"It's getting late. But what say the first thing tomorrow morning we go talk to Richard Anderson and see what he knows about our missing gentleman?"

"I think that might be real interesting," Davenport agreed.

41

Place One Condominiums is made up of older but nicely maintained units. With a facade of beige stucco and dark brown wood trim, Richard Anderson's unit number 7523-C took up the second and third floors in the middle section of his building. A smaller condo unit was beneath his on the ground floor. Staircases leading to the commodious upstairs units were separated by bottle-brush trees, and additional plantings of live oak and sabal palms had been placed around the buildings also. All in all, the neighborhood seemed a pleasant, middle-class area.

"This is the building, and . . . that's the right unit over there," Velboom said. He was driving while Steve Davenport lolled comfortably in the passenger seat. Velboom headed for a vacant parking slot.

Until Davenport lurched upright. "Don't slow down. No, don't stop. Go, go, go."

Velboom knew his partner well enough by now to first do what Steve said. Questions could come later.

Driving past the Anderson place, Velboom went to the back of the development and turned around, finally stopping in an empty stretch of parking spots.

"What's the deal, Steve?"

"Did you notice the black Regal parked back there?"

"Sure."

"Did you notice the little sticker on the back end of it?"

"No, and I didn't count the bug specks either. I take it you did?"

"Something like that." Davenport grinned. "The little sticky thing on the back says Remsgar Buick."

"And if you believe in coincidences . . ."

"Then I've got some real nice waterfront property to sell you, you bet," Davenport finished.

"And now we have a connection here with Remsgar, where our good friend Connie works."

"You know, I think it might be a nice idea if we were to find out a little more about Richard Anderson before we go marching in to speak with the man."

"I think I agree with you."

Velboom put the duty car in gear. On the way out Davenport jotted down the license tag number on the brand-new turbocharged Buick coupe.

As soon as they got back to the office, Velboom buzzed Crime Intelligence analyst Pete Monti and asked for his help. Monti would look into the Buick and into the past records, if any, of Connie Beasley and Richard Anderson. While he was doing that, Velboom and Davenport would look into the Hillsborough County arrest that Beasley was grumbling about when they talked to her.

The clerk at the Hillsborough County Sheriff's Office, after a lengthy records search, eventually produced the official report. It stated fairly little. On May 27, Beasley turned herself in, in response to a capias (arrest warrant) issued for failure to appear on a reckless driving charge. She was booked into the county jail and quickly released under bond that was automatically set at $250 for that charge. The officer who processed her at that time was unable to add any information to the sketchy report, so the FDLE agents asked to meet with the officer who initially issued the reckless driving ticket.

They met Officer John Passow of the Tampa Police Department, and he told a rather more interesting tale than the one Connie Beasley spun.

Her version of it was that the car was powerful and the road wet and she just by inattention spun around a little bit.

According to Officer Passow, on March 31, while on patrol, he observed a black Buick and a gold Corvette engaged in drag racing between traffic signals. Both cars were traveling well in excess of the speed limit, and the Buick ran a red light. Passow stopped both cars. The driver of the Buick was Connie Beasley. Passow cut her a break. He could have placed her under arrest but chose instead to simply write her a ticket, requiring her to appear in court to answer the charge. He also cited the driver of the Corvette.

"She wasn't alone in the car," Passow remembered. "There was a white male passenger. No sir, I had no reason to take any information from him, so I can't tell you who he was. I do recall, though, after I gave her the ticket the man changed places with her and was behind the wheel when they left. The license number of the Buick was . . . I have it here . . . oh, yes. The number is CTZ 23X."

Velboom and Davenport were not amazed. The number was that of the black turbo Regal parked outside Richard Anderson's condo unit. They definitely had a connection now between Connie Beasley and Richard Anderson.

But how did Robert Grantham, Connie's would-be lover, fit into the triangle? If a triangle it was, that is.

When they returned to the office, Pete Monti was still out working on the information Velboom asked for, so the agents knocked off for the day.

Early the next morning, however, Monti reported back to Velboom.

"First thing, Anderson bought the car at Remsgar Buick in Bartow on February twenty-eight. He paid just under twenty thousand for it and traded in a 1983 Olds. And if you want to know, they gave him eighty-six hundred for the Oldsmobile. The salesperson . . . do I hear drum rolls? . . . was a Ms. Connie Beasley."

"Now how is it that I'm not surprised? So what else do you have on our lovebirds, Pete?"

Monti's grin came out into the open then. "About Beasley, not much. A recent traffic violation. But just wait until you hear what we found when we checked out Richard Anderson. This is gonna knock the socks right off your feet, Ray." He laughed. "You won't even have to take your shoes off for it to happen."

42

The police report Pete Monti handed to Ray Velboom was about a hundred pages thick. It came from the St. Petersburg Police Department, across the bay from Tampa.

The pages transported him back a good fifteen years to May of 1972. The first report had to do with events on May 23, a Tuesday.

*　　*　　*

Josephine Leahy, desk clerk at the Bond Hotel in St. Petersburg, pressed a toggle on the switchboard and answered an incoming call. A man's voice asked what room James Winans was in.

"Three twenty-six. Shall I connect you?" Josephine asked.

The caller hung up.

Josephine shrugged and, glancing across the lobby, saw that it was just as well the party hadn't wanted to be rung through. Mr. Winans, elderly and frail, was seated in one of the rocking chairs on the hotel's front porch. Like many of the city's hotels, especially those that might have seen better days during past decades, the Bond had become a residence hotel catering to the aged and marginally infirm. Somewhere between a boarding house and a limited care nursing home, the residence hotels offered a measure of dignity and decency at rock-bottom monthly rates.

Josephine genuinely liked nearly all the old folks—this was 1972 and cries of Gray Power (a movement for the rights of senior citizens) were barely beginning to be heard; senior citizens could still be called old folks then without offense being taken—that she worked near at the Bond. Most of them were polite and talkative and kind to her. Mr. Winans was definitely one of the residents whom she liked.

Fifteen or so minutes later, she was not certain of the time lapse, she noticed two young men—probably in their middle thirties—pass through the lobby to the elevator. Both, she said, were tall, dressed in light gray conservative business suits and both were very tidy in their appearance. One of them wore eyeglasses with dark frames. The two gentlemen took the elevator up but returned to the lobby moments later. One of them approached the desk.

"Is James Winans around?"

Josephine pointed him out. Mr. Winans was visiting

with Nin Bond, the owner of the hotel. Just about then Bond stood and came inside. At the same time the two visitors went out onto the porch and engaged Winans in a conversation that neither Josephine nor her employer overheard.

After a brief exchange Winans and the two men left together, walking east on 4th Avenue until they were out of sight.

Two days later when Winans had not returned, Nin Bond notified the St. Petersburg Police Department that one of their guests was missing. The investigating officers found Winans's room to be tidy—and empty.

James Winans was described as being a white male sixty-nine years old, five-feet-ten, approximately 160 pounds, with thinning gray hair and wearing gold wire-rimmed glasses. Winans was also said to be a millionaire.

Some two weeks later another red flag was raised by attorney Fred Wilder, who represented James Winans's legal interests. Winans liked to stay in close contact with Wilder, and it had now been weeks since they last spoke. Wilder decided to call Winans's bank to see if they might know where the old gentleman was.

They did not. But they found it interesting that the lawyer was calling. This was the second recent call they'd had regarding James Winans, albeit a very different sort of call than the first had been.

On June 3, Wilder was told, City Bank and Trust received a call from a Joseph Golden of the North Miami Beach brokerage house H. Heintz and Co., Inc. Golden said he was considering purchasing 2,200 shares of Putnam Fund stock from Winans and wanted to inquire about Winans's financial stability before he completed the transaction.

Attorney Wilder became somewhat concerned at that point. As James Winans's lawyer he knew that his client always handled his stock trading through David Anderson of Merrill Lynch, a broker and a brokerage house that he trusted implicitly.

Wilder put through a call to Heintz and Co. and spoke with Golden, who told him that James Winans sold some $18,000 worth of securities to Heintz. A check for the full amount was mailed to Winans at the Cadillac Motel in Miami.

Increasingly alarmed, Wilder placed a call to the motel and asked to be put through to James Winans. The motel operator made a connection without delay. But the party who answered was definitely not Wilder's elderly client.

The man in Winans's room identified himself as Tom Wilson. When asked to put Winans on the line, Wilson said Winans was unavailable just then because he was in Jacksonville visiting his girlfriend. He wouldn't be back until June 12. But the caller could try back for him then.

Wilder thanked Wilson and hung up, and immediately called the St. Petersburg police.

The St. Petersburg police just as quickly passed Wilder's alert on to the authorities in Miami.

By the time the Miami police arrived at the motel, though—and very little time had passed—Winans (rather, the man posing as Winans) and Wilson had left in a hurry. The two men who had occupied the room left in such a hurry that they did not even bother to stop by the motel desk to pick up their mail. There, waiting for them in a pigeonhole, was the H. Heintz and Co. check for $18,000. The police confiscated the check and took it with them.

Further investigation found that the identification presented to Joseph Golden when the stock shares were sold was a temporary driver's license issued to James Winans, a white male six feet tall, date of birth April 15, 1944. The real James Winans was born in 1903.

Temporary license No. 670740 was issued to "Winans'' at the Florida Highway Patrol Station in Pinellas Park, Florida, a small town immediately north of St. Petersburg.

The license carried an ''A'' restriction, meaning the bearer was required to wear corrective glasses.

At about the same time, while running a routine background check on the missing James Winans, police discovered that not long earlier he had opened a checking account at Liberty National Bank in St. Petersburg, depositing $50 cash to open the account.

Within three days, however, Winans had written checks drawn against the account in amounts totaling $1,515. The checks quite naturally bounced, and the bank immediately closed the account.

The identification used when the account was opened was temporary driver's license No. 670740. The same ID used to make the stock sale in Miami.

A major break in the case came when police discovered that one particularly sharp sales clerk took down the information given on the temporary license, but also took the added precaution of jotting down the license tag number on the alleged James Winans's automobile.

That license tag was carried by a 1961 Rambler, owned by Sandra Anderson of Clearwater, Florida, yet another Pinellas County town just north of St. Petersburg.

When detectives went to her house she was not in, but her parents, with whom she was living, said if there was anything unsavory going on perhaps the police should talk with Sandra's former husband, Richard.

A day later Sandra Anderson called the detectives, indicating a willingness to help if she could. She knew nothing about any worthless check charges, she said, but if the police wanted to talk with Richard, she thought they could find him living somewhere in California. She suggested they might be able to get Richard's address from his brother, David, who was a stockbroker with Merrill Lynch.

Winans's attorney had already mentioned to them that the old gentleman's broker was David Anderson of Merrill Lynch.

Asked for a description of her ex-husband, Sandra Anderson precisely described the taller of the two men who left the Bond Hotel with James Winans on May 23. Anderson was the man in the gray suit and dark-framed eyeglasses. That description also fit the "James Winans" who checked into the Cadillac Motel in Miami. And the "James Winans" who sold 2,200 shares of Putnam to Joseph Golden. And the "James Winans" who obtained a temporary driver's license in Pinellas Park.

The St. Petersburg detectives knew—or thought they knew with a good degree of certainty—what had happened to James Winans. But they could not prove it. The case went onto a shelf—open but not active.

Their second major break in the spring of 1973, when the St. Petersburg detectives received a call from a special agent with the Federal Bureau of Investigation in California. Did they have an unsolved murder or disappearance involving an elderly man? Yes, they did. No body had ever been found, but it was certainly believed that James Winans had been murdered after he disappeared from the Bond Hotel almost a year earlier.

A man named Patrick Johnson, the FBI agent said, just walked in off the street and confessed to the crime.

Johnson had recently joined the Jews for Jesus movement in San Francisco. Because of his new religious conviction, he felt while he had already made his peace with God, he still was obligated to make peace with society. Confessing to his past transgression was the right thing to do, and he would not be able to fully rest until it was done. He wanted to tell the police about the murder. What he had done, and what his partner had done.

Johnson was flown from San Francisco to St. Petersburg and was met at the airport by expecting detectives, who drove him directly to the Bond Hotel.

Without being either questioned or prompted, Patrick Johnson immediately identified the building as the one from which James Winans was abducted. He said the car he and his partner used had been parked around the corner from the hotel.

Satisfied that Johnson's story was checking out, the detectives took their voluntary suspect to the fourth floor interview room at the police department headquarters.

Johnson told them that his partner was Richard Anderson. He first met Anderson when both men lived in San Francisco. They became friends, and when Anderson said he wanted to move back to Florida, Johnson said he wanted to go along. While taking in the sights at Boulder Dam, Johnson said, Anderson told him he knew of an old man who had bales of stocks. And if Johnson would kill him, Anderson thought they could net a good hundred thousand dollars or so off the old fellow.

The money sounded good, Johnson said, and he agreed to do the killing if Anderson set up the target.

When they got to Florida, Richard Anderson called the trailer park where James Winans used to live and was told that he had moved to the Bond Hotel. No, he said, he did not know David Anderson, and in fact remembered Richard saying that his brother was not to find out that he was in town because he didn't want David able to make any connection between Richard, who knew about James Winans's wealth, and Winans's as yet unaccomplished disappearance.

Johnson's story of the events at the Bond Hotel exactly matched those told the year before by Josephine Leahy and Nin Bond—the telephone call, the trip up in the elevator and inquiry at the desk, and finally the brief conversation on the front porch.

According to Johnson, he and Anderson introduced themselves as mobile home salesmen who wanted to interest Winans in investment properties. They talked the old man into accompanying them to look at some mobiles for sale.

Using that pretext the three walked around the corner and got into Anderson's 1967 Oldsmobile Cutlass. Anderson drove, Winans rode in the front passenger seat, and Johnson was in back. While they drove they talked to Winans about financial arrangements in the event a deal should be concluded, and found out where he did his banking.

Johnson said Anderson pulled onto a dirt road just north of a major intersection and drove a few hundred yards down the dirt track before stopping.

"He told the old guy this was where a mobile home park was going to be built and he should look it over."

Winans got out of the car to look at the property, and Richard Anderson bent down and got a gun from beneath the seat of his car. He handed the gun to Johnson, who stepped out of the car and approached Winans.

Aged and unable to run away, James Winans saw what was happening but was not physically able to prevent it.

He stood there with his head up, looking straight at his own murderer, and "took it like a man," Johnson said.

Johnson shot Winans once in the head, and probably was dead by the time he hit the ground.

Anderson and Johnson searched the body for the key to Winans's safe-deposit box but were unable to find anything. They did, however, take the key to his room at the Bond.

Leaving the body where it was, Anderson and Johnson drove back into the city and, waiting until dinnertime, when there would be no one at the front desk, Anderson slipped unseen into Winans's room, where he located the safe deposit key he wanted.

They went to the Mid County Commercial Bank,

where Anderson used the key and false ID to gain admission to James Winans's lockbox. He took the stock certificates he found there, and he and Johnson drove together to Miami, where they checked into the Cadillac Motel.

Anderson made the deal with Joseph Golden, and, while waiting for the money on the sale to be delivered, left Johnson at the motel while he went back to St. Petersburg to tend to some unspecified business.

That was when attorney Wilder called the motel room. Afraid that things had gone terribly wrong, Patrick Johnson wiped the motel room clean of any fingerprints and fled, heading for St. Petersburg, where he was able to reestablish contact with Richard Anderson.

Disappointed that they had not struck it rich after all, the two decided to put Florida behind them. They drifted back to California.

After some thought and a few false starts, Patrick Johnson was able to lead police to the empty field where the killing occurred. Although it had been almost a year since the murder, there were still some human bones to be found at the scene. The one piece of evidence most useful for the purposes of identification, the skull, was missing, however. Detectives assumed some animal had dragged the skull away, and it was unlikely it would ever be recovered after so long.

With Patrick Johnson comfortably ensconced in jail, the detectives had no trouble locating Richard Anderson, even though he had moved to Orlando and was living under the name George Ehmig.

Anderson was taken into custody and, far from claiming he was falsely accused, very quickly agreed to give a statement that basically corroborated the confession given by Patrick Johnson.

One thing Anderson added that Johnson had not known was that when he left Johnson in the Miami mo-

tel room and returned to St. Petersburg, it was because
he did not trust Johnson to remain silent.

To guard against James Winans's body being identified, Anderson went back to the murder scene and removed Winans's head from his body, carrying it to
another location and hiding it.

Anderson agreed to take detectives to this second site,
where indeed a human skull was recovered. The skull
was later identified by way of dental records as being
that of James Winans.

Patrick Johnson pleaded no contest to a charge of
first-degree murder on July 3, 1973. He was sentenced
to life in prison.

On May 29, 1974, Richard Anderson entered a guilty
plea to first-degree murder and was sentenced to serve
six months to twenty years in prison. Eight years later,
in August 1982, he was released.

Ray Velboom stared with fascination at the volumi-
nous report in his hands. He read over and over again
one very small and seemingly insignificant entry that
appeared within those many pages. Part of Richard Anderson's statement after his arrest, the note that so cap-
tivated Velboom's attention these many years later, was
this:

Worried about the possibility that they may have been
seen with James Winans in the car and afraid that the
car might therefore be used to identify them as murder-
ers, Richard Anderson insisted on flying back to California after first getting rid of his Oldsmobile. He did
this *by abandoning it in the Tampa International Airport
parking lot.* Same man, same method.

Ray Velboom felt secure in his own mind that there
was no longer any need to pursue Robert Grantham as
a man in hiding. Grantham, Velboom was now convinced, was Richard Anderson's second murder victim.

And very likely for the same reason as the first murder was committed: greed.

After all, poor stupid Lyin' Bob had called half the people he ever knew to tell them how much he was winning in Vegas, so much that he was afraid for his safety.

Well, apparently he'd had more reason than he even knew to worry about that.

And perhaps the saddest part of it was that it did not even matter this time if Lyin' Bob was telling the truth about his big score in Las Vegas. So long as someone— say, Connie Beasley for example—believed he had a huge wad of cash in his pockets, then he was setting himself up as a target. He might just as well have had a bull's-eye drawn on his back in bright, bold colors.

A target within a triangle if one wanted to look at it that way, Velboom thought. And the points of the triangle were Robert Grantham, with his penchant for bragging about how much money he carried; Connie Beasley, who had what Bob Grantham so earnestly wanted and who was said to do almost anything for money; and Richard Anderson, who once before in the past killed a man in the hope of garnering some cash.

Velboom's problem now was the same one those St. Petersburg detectives faced fifteen years earlier. He pretty much knew what happened, to whom and by whom. But he did not yet have evidence that a prosecutor could take to a jury.

Velboom laid the St. Petersburg police report aside and dialed the FDLE duty officer. He asked her to get hold of Steve Davenport.

43

Steve Davenport and Ray Velboom were acutely aware that Florida law generally precludes a jury from hearing testimony about any previous criminal activity. Anderson's previous murder conviction could not be used to show that having done it once he most likely did it again.

The State Attorney's office confirmed this when the FDLE agents consulted with the prosecutors about the feasibility of filing charges against Anderson.

That murder—even the fact that the car used that time was abandoned at Tampa International Airport—was not sufficient cause to arrest Anderson much less bring him to trial. The prosecutors emphasized that even if Anderson could be charged at some time in the future, they would not so much as attempt to bring the facts of the previous murder before the jury, since its use would taint the prosecution's case to such an extent that afterward it would probably lead to a reversal by the Florida Supreme Court.

What Davenport and Velboom were told by the State's Attorney was that they needed to develop further evidence that would prove their case.

The first and best such evidence would, of course, be the body of Robert T. Grantham, since at this point it was still an assumption, albeit a reasonable one, that the missing man was dead.

Just to make sure all bases were covered, the agents went to the Pinellas County site where the body of James Winans had been dumped and then to the secondary site, where Winans's skull was discarded. Both locations were thoroughly searched, but nothing was found.

They next obtained Anderson's prison files to see if there was anything they could glean from those. There was very little of interest and nothing of benefit. Anderson was the youngest of five children; he had been born in Alabama but moved often in his youth because his father was in the navy. Most of the man's life had been remarkably uneventful, except for his occasional lapse into murder.

Now with the easy-to-reach plums having already been picked, the agents took up the tedious grind of hard, patient leg work. They obtained driver's license photographs of all three likely participants in the events of the night of May 7—Robert Grantham, Richard Anderson, and Connie Beasley—and began showing the photos to employees at Orlando Airport.

Lisa Weyngarden was working at the boarding gate when Grantham's TranStar Airlines flight arrived that afternoon. She could not recall having seen any of the three that day. TranStar employee Allan Boyd, who was also on duty at Gate 10 that afternoon, said that he thought Grantham looked familiar and that Connie Beasley may have picked Grantham up; but he was not sure.

They interviewed skycap Willie Johnson, who handled the only request for wheelchair assistance that afternoon. Johnson seemed reluctant to become involved and said he took someone to a Park 'n Ride bus, but he could not recall whether it was Grantham he transported.

They talked with Park 'n Ride supervisor Sidney McLaughlin, and through him were able to talk with all the bus drivers who worked on May 7, but none were able to recognize anyone in the photographs.

However, one driver, Robert Meindel, remembered one passenger on a bus run he made who bragged about winning twenty thousand dollars in Las Vegas. The man was loud, he said, and boisterous. Steve Davenport thought that alone was enough to positively identify the passenger as Robert Grantham. Except, that is, for purposes of testimony.

While they were busy in Orlando, a similar search was undertaken at Tampa International, using the help of special agent Sam Jones. In addition to showing the photographs to everyone he could think of, Jones also checked to see if there was any unclaimed luggage belonging to Grantham. He further talked with the airport housekeeping services personnel to find out if any bloody clothing was found during the first week of May.

Jones's efforts were no more revealing than the Orlando canvass had been. No one at either location could positively say that Robert Grantham was there much less either of the two suspects, Richard Anderson and Connie Beasley.

In addition to working the airports in search of witnesses, agents Velboom and Davenport, assisted by other FDLE agents, as work schedules permitted, began conducting a sporadic surveillance of both Anderson and Beasley.

Their hope, improbable though it was, was that Anderson might again decide to return to the place where he had disposed of a body so he could tidy up loose ends.

They were, of course, disappointed.

On the other hand, they several times observed the two suspects together, confirming the fact that a relationship did indeed exist between Anderson and Beasley.

They also observed that Anderson spent time daily at Tampa Forklift. They assumed he worked there, but the agents did not want to reveal their surveillance by talking to supervisory personnel at the company. Better, they thought, to wait, since the question of Anderson's employment was not nearly so important as that the suspect remain unaware that he was under scrutiny.

In order to further corroborate the relationship, the agents requested a pen register, which is a device that records the numbers to which outgoing telephone calls are placed.

On June 11, 1987, the Hon. Susan Sexton, a circuit judge in Tampa, reviewed the application and signed an order allowing its placement on the telephone line assigned to Anderson.

That afternoon Special Agent Supervisor E.J. Picolo met with General Telephone security agents Brent Provoncha and Karen Eichenbacker, and the device was installed. The very first call made from Anderson's residence afterward was placed to a number that was already familiar to the agents, the home of Maurice Gilliard, where Connie Beasley and her children were living with Connie's parents.

More calls were recorded to the Gilliard residence through the duration of the pen register emplacement.

But all the register could do was verify that a relationship existed between Anderson and Beasley. Much more than that was needed before they could even think about arrests.

Maybe in Las Vegas . . .

44

Steve Davenport was unable to make the trip, so special agent Scotty Sanderson drew the dubious pleasure of accompanying Velboom to America's desert gambling haven.

They arrived at Las Vegas's McCarran Airport in a searing midday heat that even Florida's climate could not prepare them for.

Bypassing the allure of the slot machines inside the airport, Velboom and Sanderson headed immediately for the Fremont Hotel, where Grantham had been booked during his last visit to the city.

There they spoke with manager Theresa Johnson. She had no trouble producing a room registration card that verified Grantham's visit. He checked in exactly as scheduled on May 4 and checked out the morning of May 7 for his (fateful) return to Orlando.

Beyond that, though, Ms. Johnson could not help. Neither she nor the desk clerk who had been on duty at the time Grantham registered could remember him from among the many other guests who had passed through the hotel since that time. His photo triggered no recognition, nor could any of the hotel personnel recall if Grantham might have been accompanied by

160

anyone else, male or female, during his visit.

From the Fremont the agents proceeded to the Las Vegas Police Department, where they met a sympathetic and cooperative, but unfortunately informationless, detective, Bill Wilson.

"About all I can suggest," Wilson offered, "is the same thing you'd do if you were at home. Walk." He grinned. "Take your photos and start talking to employees in all the casinos your man may have visited."

Sanderson groaned playfully and gave the local detective a smile.

"I'll tell you what I can do," Wilson offered. "It's a long shot, but all casinos are obliged to contact us when a person files for a gambling credit line. Let me take down the information on your guy and I'll run him through the computer."

"We'd appreciate it."

"It will only take a few minutes. Help yourselves to some coffee while you're waiting. I'll be right back."

It was too hot for coffee. But at least the wait was in air-conditioned comfort.

Det. Wilson was smiling when he returned. "We have a match. Your guy Grantham applied for a credit line at the Four Queens Casino. By the way, I ran Anderson while I was at it. We come up empty on him."

"You're a gentleman and a scholar, Wilson." Velboom thought about something and shook his head. "That poor, stupid damn Grantham. Lyin' Bob, indeed."

"Pardon me?"

"LBG, that's his nickname. And no wonder. He was telling everyone back home about all his huge winnings. So much so that it probably got him killed. Yet he had to ask for credit at the Four Queens so he could play."

Wilson grunted. After a moment he said, "Come on, gents. I'll take you over to the Four Queens and we'll see if we can develop anything there."

Despite the friendly local's help, though, no one at

the Four Queens recognized either Robert Grantham or
Richard Anderson.

Velboom and Sanderson spent the next several days
laboriously hiking from casino to casino, showing the
photos to every dealer, bartender, or waitress they en-
countered.

No one recognized either man. Finally, every avenue
that they could think of exhausted, they gave up the
search in Las Vegas and returned to Florida, where,
looking for a fresh point of view, they asked Steve
Brady[1] to enter the case.

45

My name is Steve Brady, and I am the Regional Legal
Advisor for the Florida Department of Law Enforcement
in Orlando. Besides Orlando we have field attorneys in
Tallahassee, Jacksonville, Miami, and Tampa. Our role
is to provide legal assistance to special agents during the
course of their investigations. This is necessary because
law enforcement has become so complicated, due to
court rulings pertaining to the constitutional rights of
suspects, that it is difficult for cops to function without
the services of a lawyer. Therefore, most major police
agencies in Florida have attorneys on staff.

It was in that capacity one afternoon in June of 1987

---

[1] Attorney Steve Brady is one of the co-authors of this work.

that I was helping an agent put together a search warrant when the telephone in my office rang. Excusing myself, I picked up the receiver and heard Ray Velboom's voice.

At that time, the attorney in the Tampa office had recently resigned and I was filling in while a replacement was being sought, so it was not unusual for me to get calls from the West Coast offices asking for legal advice.

When I told Ray Velboom that I was in the process of reviewing a search warrant affidavit, he hurriedly summarized his case and asked if they could legally attempt one avenue that until now had not been pursued.

The request he put before me was so unorthodox for a murder investigation—but at the same time so intriguing—that I told him I would come to Tampa as soon as I could, the following day at the very latest, to discuss his plan with him.

When I reached the Tampa office the next morning, Steve Davenport and Ray Velboom were waiting for me. They quickly recapped what the investigation had uncovered thus far, and then proposed what they thought was the only viable way to solve the crime.

The agents wanted to intercept telephone conversations between Richard Anderson and Connie Beasley, in the hope of hearing them discuss the murder.

A basically good idea, but with a legal catch: In order to obtain a court order authorizing a wire intercept, it is required that sufficient probable cause be established to show that a crime has been or is being committed. In this case, I conceded that there was more than ample probable cause to believe a murder had occurred and, additionally, that Richard Anderson and Connie Beasley had been involved in the commission of that murder.

But that was not the extent of what would be required to obtain a wire intercept authorization.

In addition to probable cause, there must also be a reasonable expectation, in fact an actual likelihood, that conversations regarding the event will take place during the course of the intercept.

In other words, the courts will not authorize fishing expeditions.

Largely because of this I had never heard of an intercept being approved in anything other than investigations involving ongoing criminal enterprises, activities such as gambling or drug dealing, when it is common for the co-conspirators to call each other on a regular basis to talk business.

This case was obviously very different from that norm. The pen register already showed that Anderson and Beasley spoke frequently, but there was nothing on record to indicate that they had been or would be discussing Robert Grantham over the telephone. The two suspects had a boyfriend/girlfriend relationship in which it would be considered normal for them to speak with each other frequently. And, anyway, it had already been more than a month since Robert Grantham's Thunderbird was discovered abandoned at the airport in Tampa. By now, Anderson and Beasley would probably feel that they had literally gotten away with murder.

It was my best judgment at the time that no judge was likely to authorize a wire intercept on the basis of the information that had been given to me. So I advised the agents against making an application.

If there is one thing that can be said about the Florida Department of Law Enforcement, though, it is that its personnel can be both very innovative and tenaciously persistent. My rejection of their plan at this point was taken not as a turndown but as a challenge.

Because an interception of communications between Anderson and Beasley might well be the only realistic method for bringing the two to justice, the idea of a wiretap approval did not die. It merely fermented.

During several days of long and intense debate, a

scheme was conceived that was simply put, quite brilliant.

In order to create a reasonable likelihood that the murder would be discussed over the telephone, what the agents proposed was a perfectly legal nudge in that direction.

If the wire intercept were authorized, they planned, FDLE agents would wait until it was installed and then immediately approach Connie Beasley at her place of work. There they would confront her with a statement saying they believed Richard Anderson murdered her would-be paramour, Robert Grantham.

If she denied being involved in the murder—as was, of course, anticipated—the agents would leave. Once they were gone it could reasonably be assumed that Beasley would call Anderson to warn him that he was a suspect in Grantham's disappearance. And the wire intercept would be in place to record that conversation.

If on the other hand Beasley admitted complicity and confessed to being a participant in the crime, the agents would immediately terminate the intercept and ask the court to rescind the authorization order.

And in order to provide a contingency in the event Beasley chose to drive to Anderson's residence to deliver her warning, a listening device would also be secreted within the condominium unit as part of the same intercept order.

After reviewing the agents' plans, I determined that this revised version of their initial request would pass judicial muster, and I was pleased to be able to give them a green light.

Ray Velboom and Steve Davenport immediately began scrambling to put together the twenty-two-page document that was required to apply for a judicial order authorizing the interception of communications between Richard Anderson and Connie Beasley.

In addition to my in-house approval, the agents were

required to run their application through the State Attorney's office, in this instance, through Hillsborough County prosecutor Lee Atkinson; and, once past him, through State Attorney Bill James as well.

Working up the line to secure the necessary sign-offs, the agents eventually arrived before Circuit Court Judge Susan Sexton, the same judge who earlier approved use of the pen register on Richard Anderson's telephone line.

After a thorough review of the documents and accompanying approvals, Judge Sexton asked, "When do you anticipate confronting Ms. Beasley?"

"Today, if we can get up on the wire," Velboom responded.

The judge nodded and asked if they had an order prepared ready for her signature. Velboom gave the written order to Lee Atkinson, who passed it to the judge.

She looked it over and signed it.

"Good luck, gentlemen."

The date was July 1, 1987, slightly less than two months since Robert Grantham returned from his Las Vegas vacation.

46

FDLE surveillance teams had been in place well before Judge Sexton was approached with the wire intercept request, starting at 6:45, when special agent Debbie Crosby took up station across the road from Tampa Forklift, where Anderson was employed.

She could not spot the black Buick, however, nor could the agents who were positioned outside Anderson's condo. With none of the agents able to determine Anderson's whereabouts, they placed a call to his home to find out if he was in. Had he picked up, the agent on the line would have apologized for reaching a wrong number. As it happened, though, the telephone went unanswered. Richard Anderson finally showed up at his home at 11:41 A.M., the time that was logged by special agent Roger Martindill. Forty minutes later Anderson came back outside and drove away, with a team of FDLE personnel trailing unobtrusively behind.

Anderson drove east. Anderson's stop in Bartow was Remsgar Buick, where Connie Beasley was on duty on the showroom floor.

Certain that they would not be interrupted, and with Judge Sexton's authorization signed and delivered, Special Agent Supervisor Larry Sams led an entry team into Anderson's condominium.

Once inside they installed and carefully hid an audio listening device that would pick up and transmit the voices of any occupants speaking inside the dwelling. The receiver was located back at the FDLE Tampa office. After a test to make sure everything was working properly, the entry team took one last look to insure nothing had been visibly disturbed. Then they quietly left. The entry and installation had taken less than half an hour.

While Sams's team was busy inside the condo, another team of agents, working together with security personnel from the telephone company, hooked up the equipment necessary for the telephone wire intercept. That, too, was accomplished while Anderson was at Remsgar Buick.

When he left the auto dealership Anderson made several other stops, presumably business related, in Polk County. He stopped at a citrus processing plant on Home Juice Road, at a candy company on US 27, and at several other locations.

Throughout his daily travels, although he did not know it, he was accompanied by FDLE agents who observed and recorded his movements. Anderson finally returned home at 4:50 P.M.

Even then, however, the agents exhibited patience, not willing to activate the intercept instruments until they were reasonably sure that Anderson was in to stay. It would have been a disaster if they timed the approach to Beasley—and pinned their hopes for a successful conclusion to the case on her reactions—just about the time Anderson might decide to leave home for a hamburger.

They waited until past seven o'clock before taking the plunge.

It had already been decided that with so much riding on the talk with Beasley, it would be a good idea for a supervisor to be involved in the "re-interview" that they hoped would flush their quarry.

Manny Pondakos, the same special agent supervisor who originally spotted the blood-soaked Thunderbird at Tampa International, accompanied Ray Velboom for the critically important confrontation.

The two agents entered Remsgar at 7:25 P.M. and told Beasley they wanted to talk to her again. On advice from Steve Brady, they deliberately avoided reading her the list of Miranda rights. The rationale was that since she would not be in custody, the elaboration of her rights was not strictly necessary—not yet, anyway. And if they tried to play it safe and read the Miranda list, she might well decide to remain silent—which, of course, would ruin everything.

Beasley seemed reluctant to talk to the agents, but she agreed on condition she could have a witness present during the conversation. Velboom and Pondakos quickly agreed, and Beasley went to find the dealership's business manager, Edward Cullaro. Cullaro invited the agents and Beasley into his office, where they would not be interrupted.

Velboom began by telling Beasley something she already knew—and in fact had herself already told them about—that Grantham's telephone records showed he placed several calls to Remsgar Buick while he was in Las Vegas, and in addition made one call to Beasley from Houston where he had a brief layover.

Beasley's expression remained neutral.

Velboom next added that the telephone record showed a call made to Rudy Benton from a residence in Tampa. Beasley had not known about that, and this time her eyes narrowed, but her expression remained frozen.

Pondakos gave Velboom a "go for the throat" stare and Velboom calmly said, "That call was made from a condominium belonging to Richard Anderson. Do you know Richard Anderson?"

Beasley's facade was beginning to crack. She hesitated, then nodded. She had met him, she admitted. He came by the dealership in February to look at a car. And yes, they were dating now. But she knew nothing about any telephone call or why Robert Grantham would have been in Richard's home. Why, as far as she knew, Bob Grantham and her boyfriend Richard didn't even know each other.

"Richard Anderson had been convicted of murder once already. You know that, don't you?"

It was a question Connie Beasley never did answer. She seemed too stunned to speak. Velboom noticed that the revelation certainly got Ed Cullaro's attention, too.

Neither Velboom nor Pondakos said anything more for several very long and silent moments, as the pressures that were surely building inside Connie Beasley had time to develop.

Beasley said nothing either. She mutely shook her head several times and shrugged her shoulders.

Velboom and Pondakos stood, their expressions hard. "We may want to talk to you again later. Good-bye."

As soon as they reached their car outside, Pondakos picked up the cellular phone and called the wire tap "listening post," where Steve Davenport was waiting.

With the signal to activate the system coming from Pondakos, Davenport turned to the technician handling the equipment and nodded. "Turn it on."

The wait for Beasley's call to be put through to Richard Anderson's telephone was, literally, a matter of seconds.

The intercept was brought on-line barely in time to record the ensuing conversation.

47

"Hello." It was Richard Anderson's voice.

"Can you hear me?"

"Yeah."

"Get a ticket and get out of town." Connie Beasley sounded breathless, very agitated.

"What?"

"Get a ticket and get out of town. Do you understand me?"

"Hold on. What are you saying?"

"I'm just saying that they know everything."

"What?"

"They think that you . . . did that."

"Why?"

"Because they do . . . they got. . . ."

"They got what?"

"Ed and Mr. Remsgar . . . they all know everything . . . they know about your murders before . . . they got all the proof . . . they are down there with mom and dad right now."

"Your mom's house?"

"Yeah. Get out of town, Richard!"

"All right . . . you for real?"

"I'm . . . Richard . . . Ed's here . . . they are all here. . . . ''

"All right."

"Don't ever come back," she implored.

"Are you for real?" Anderson sounded bemused. But then the warning was still new to him, apparently stunning in its impact.

"Richard . . ."

"Have they found anything?"

"Uh . . . uh huh . . . listen to me. . . . ''

"What?"

"They . . . they . . . I'm just telling you, they're coming. They're coming to your place. . . . ''

"Yeah?"

". . . now!"

"All right. Bye."

48

Special agent William Miles had been monitoring the intercept. As soon as Beasley and Anderson disconnected, Miles called Bureau Chief Ed Williams and Supervisor E. J. Picolo to tell them that Velboom's and Davenport's ploy had succeeded.

Picolo immediately passed that information along to Manny Pondakos, who, along with the other agents on the Beasley surveillance team, was still outside the auto dealership in Bartow. He and Ray Velboom, barely able to suppress their excitement, agreed that the telephone warning to Anderson would constitute probable cause for the arrest of Connie Beasley.

They met her already on her way out to make her own break, almost running into her as she tried to exit the building while they were headed back into it. Her eyes widened in sudden alarm, and she seemed to Velboom like an animal caught in the glare of headlights from an onrushing car. She froze, immobilized in place as she was reaching for the door Manny Pondakos had just opened.

It was Ray Velboom's pleasure to make the announcement that Beasley no doubt was dreading. "Ms. Beasley, at this time I am placing you under arrest for being an accessory after the fact to first-degree murder."

Beasley, dazed and seemingly uncertain of what was happening, docilely allowed herself to be handcuffed and led to Velboom's car.

Inside Remsgar Buick all business had come to a stop, and there was an eerie silence in the showroom as all eyes were fixed on Connie Beasley and the FDLE agents.

Manny Pondakos advised Beasley of her rights as outlined in the Miranda warnings.

In a dull, wooden voice Beasley blurted, "He did it. Richard did it. I know about the killing. I know. . . ." The voice trailed away into silence.

By then she was inside the car, Velboom guiding her carefully into the backseat so that she would not bump her head on the inside car roof.

"We'll talk to you about this when we get back to the office," he said.

If Beasley heard what was said, she did nothing to indicate that she did. She sat quiescent as if in a fog.

Velboom called in to advise the supervisors in Tampa that Beasley was in custody and that the agents with her were transporting her to Tampa for questioning.

While Velboom and Pondakos were busy with Beasley, other members of the Beasley team were already beginning the interview process with Beasley's suddenly former coworkers.

Agents David Hauser and David West spoke with Edward Cullaro, the Remsgar business manager who minutes earlier was Beasley's witness while she talked with Pondakos and Velboom.

Cullaro told them that Beasley had confided in him after she was interviewed the first time by Velboom and Davenport. At that time, Cullaro said, Beasley admitted that she knew Robert Grantham, but she assured him that she knew nothing about the Winter Haven man's disappearance.

The manager also said that Beasley was a below-average salesperson, who recently had been placed on probation because of her bad work habits and poor productivity. Asked if he knew whether she owned any firearms, Cullaro said he did not know. He volunteered, however, that he owned a .22 handgun, which he kept in the office hidden inside a bank bag. He added that the gun stayed in his possession at all times and that Beasley could not have had access to it. The agents asked Cullaro to surrender the gun for ballistics testing anyway, which he did. Lab tests later proved that Cullaro's was not the murder weapon.

In Bartow, Connie Beasley was safely in custody within minutes, and the continuing work of the investigation was well in progress.

All was not so simple in Tampa, however.

49

The Anderson surveillance team was still in place outside his condo, as it had been all day. Advised by radio that the expected call from Beasley had been made, the agents were told as well that if Anderson fled they should follow him, but that they should make no attempt to take him into custody until, or unless, Bureau Chief Ed Williams approved the arrest. Williams and Picolo were busy evaluating the taped conversation between Anderson and Beasley to make sure grounds for an arrest could be garnered from it.

Inside the condo Anderson was in such a hurry to heed Connie Beasley's advice that he left his supper on the range with the burner still on. She had said to get out, and he was intent on doing exactly that.

Grabbing nothing but his keys, Richard Anderson quit his apartment, coming into the view of the waiting FDLE agents as soon as he opened his front door.

The fox was leaving its covert and did not know the hounds were already waiting to take up the chase.

When Anderson cranked up his Buick and drove away, it took some restraint for the team of agents to refrain from all jumping in line behind him. But then forming a train would be a dead giveaway and would certainly spook the quarry. Better to lay back and co-ordinate the caravan by radio so that the tail cars could change places frequently and keep Anderson from spotting his pursuers.

Five minutes later there were three cars in close contact with Anderson, driven by agents Richard Pyles, Patricia Rodgers, and Randy Dey. An order crackled over the radio: The arrest was a go. Take him down.

Slapping portable blue police emergency lights onto their dashboards and hitting their sirens, the agents pulled in close behind Anderson.

Instead of stopping, the panicked suspect hit his accelerator and the turbocharged Buick leaped forward.

The chain of cars, three with lights and blaring sirens and one driven in desperation, careened through the streets of north Tampa.

Pyles gave his car all he had and managed to pull alongside Anderson's black Buick.

Anderson cut his wheel hard left, deliberately swerving his car toward Pyles's in an attempt to force the agent off the road.

Undaunted and unyielding, Richard Pyles held his ground, refusing to flinch away from Anderson's bumper-car tactics. Then he eased his own wheel to the right, edging the Buick onto the shoulder and off the pavement, where Anderson's car went into a slide.

Overcorrecting, sawing frantically at the wheel now, Anderson turned a slide into a spin, the Buick swapping end for end in a cascade of dirt and flying grass. The Buick spun two, perhaps three times before it came to a rocking halt.

By that time the FDLE agents had Anderson boxed in with their cars. With guns drawn and expressions intense, they ordered Anderson out of his car and advised him that he was under arrest.

Randy Dey handcuffed Anderson and transported him to the Tampa field office, where an interrogation was attempted. Anderson refused to talk, so he was taken to the Hillsborough County jail, where he was booked in on a charge of first-degree murder.

His car was impounded and taken to the crime lab for inventory and analysis, although nothing was found in that car that proved to be of interest.

While that act was being played out, back at the FDLE office Ray Velboom had the extreme satisfaction of calling Kenneth Grantham to tell him his brother's killer was in custody. Velboom asked Grantham to notify Jacquelyn O'Hara, Robin Boney, and the other parties who had been concerned about the disappearance of Bob Grantham.

There was, of course, still a great deal of work to be done. As Velboom knew much better than Grantham's family members possibly could, an arrest is one thing. It is quite another to obtain a conviction by way of trial before a jury.

It was toward that end that the FDLE agents now had to concentrate their efforts.

50

The first-degree murder trial of Richard Harold Anderson opened on February 8, 1988, some nine months after the death of Robert T. Grantham.

Presumed death, that is, especially in the view of defense counsel. Because in all the ensuing months of interrogation and investigation no body had ever been found to prove beyond question that Grantham was indeed dead.

And as the prosecution team was all too well aware, it would be a rarity of extreme degree if they were to succeed in gaining a conviction in a capital murder case—and the State's Attorney did indeed intend to seek the death penalty—when there was no body to present in evidence.

Something else prosecutors John Skye and Lee Cannon knew, which most laymen do not, is that there is very little on this green earth that is more *boring* than a real life murder trial.

The reason for this is actually quite logical and sensible. Virtually every murder conviction is subject to the intense scrutiny of appeals procedures afterward. And neither the trial judge nor the prosecution has any desire to see his or her efforts overturned by an appellate court after the fact.

Accordingly, murder trials proceed with all the swift-rushing pace of a somnolent sloth. Every procedural "i" must be carefully dotted and each technical "t" crossed and double checked and likely crossed again. The simplest and most obvious of details must be explored, examined, explained, and then presented anew from another angle.

And all this is true in the most normal of capital trials. In this case, all those norms existed, including the added burden of trying to convince a jury that a man was dead, even though there was no body to point to and, worse, when the missing and presumed dead man had quite voluntarily disappeared in the course of his own shady past.

Skye and Cannon knew they had their work cut out for them when Anderson's trial opened before Circuit Judge M. William Graybill in a small courtroom housed in the Hillsborough County Courthouse in downtown Tampa.

Skye, felony bureau chief for the Hillsborough County State Attorney's office, was the lead prosecutor. A courtroom veteran, Skye rarely lost a case. With rugged facial features topped off by salt-and-pepper hair, he had a courtroom presence that commanded a jury's attention. It was not surprising that he would have been chosen to handle this difficult prosecution.

After seating a jury of twelve, plus two alternates who would not actually deliberate unless one or more of the primary jurors had to withdraw, the prosecution team began building the case against Anderson with slow and methodical certainty.

They laid their case up carefully, like brickmasons who had to work without mortar. One mislaid piece and the entire structure could crumble, so they worked with deliberation, starting with Special Agent Supervisor Manny Pondakos, who first noticed the blood-smeared Thunderbird on a morning the previous May, and continuing with witness by witness by painstaking witness. Who saw what, who did what, who photographed what, who could assure the jury that no evidence had been altered, lost, or tampered with.

The defense team of William Fuente and Mark Ober participated very little in these highly technical opening sallies. Their expertise would come into play soon enough.

And so it did.

The first clash came when Skye called as a prosecution witness Winter Haven attorney John Kaylor, a lawyer specializing in workmen's compensation cases. Kaylor had represented Robert Grantham with the workmen's compensation claim Grantham made following his accident, and his purpose before this jury was obvious. The state wanted to show by way of Kaylor that Grantham had more than $80,000 worth of reason for *not* disappearing when he did. It was at this point that the prosecution and the defense began their technical sparring before Judge Graybill.

The prosecution wanted to imply, by way of Kaylor and other witnesses yet to come, that only death could have kept Robert Grantham out of sight so long. The defense wanted just as fervently to keep open the idea that somehow, somewhere, Lyin' Bob Grantham might still be alive, because if that could be true, then a case could be built to claim that Richard Anderson had not committed a murder the previous May.

Judge Graybill ruled in favor of the prosecution, and the case droned painstakingly forward witness by witness by witness.

Then, however, the fireworks began, preceded by the statement, ''The State calls Connie Beasley.''

51

John Skye gave the witness a moment to become comfortable in the witness box, then asked, ''Ma'am, would you please state your full name?''

Clearing her throat, she softly said, ''Connie Beasley.''

''Ms. Beasley, do you know a person by the name of Richard Anderson?''

Every single person in the courtroom except those at the defense table leaned forward with obvious expectation. Beasley, confronting Anderson for the first time since they were arrested, slowly turned from the jury and directed her attention to the defendant. Anderson's eyes narrowed as he glared back at her. Beasley flinched. But answered the question. "Yes, I do."

"How long have you known Mr. Anderson?"

"I've known him for a year."

"Would you look around and tell us if you see him in the courtroom?"

Beasley nodded in the direction of the defendant and said, "Yes, I do. He's the one sitting on the end with the reddish suit and the glasses and the tie which is blue and red."

"When did you first meet Mr. Anderson?"

Returning her attention to the jury and Skye, she said, "I met him in February of last year at Remsgar Buick and Pontiac in Bartow where I worked. He came by to look at cars. He bought one and . . . we also began to date."

"And by the time of late April, early May, how would you describe your relationship with Mr. Anderson?"

"I was very much in love with him."

Some of the jurors cast sideways glances at Anderson while others sat back in their chairs as if preparing for what they believed would be a long but very interesting story.

Connie Beasley was in love. Richard was wonderful, tall and handsome. And so energetic and commanding in bed that he positively made her giddy. Living with her parents and with two children underfoot, Connie made the trip to Richard's Tampa townhouse three or four times each week. When she stayed overnight her parents took care of her children, so she did not have that to worry about.

Better yet, Richard had spoken several times about the possibility of marriage. Not tomorrow perhaps, but soon. The prospect pleased her.

Right now everything was pleasing her. Even the weather, which had warmed up enough that she could enjoy luxuriating in the sunshine by the pool at Richard's condominium complex. She lay face down on a lounge chair with her bikini bra strap unhooked, conscious that she was attracting the attention of more than just Richard. She was just as good looking in her way as Richard was in his, and she liked being appreciated by men. Well, by most men.

Drowsy and content in the heat she opened one eye and took a long, slow look at Richard's sleek torso. There was a thin sheen of sweat on it. That turned her on. She stretched, cat-like and contented.

"Hey," she said.

"Mmm?"

"Did I tell you about the jerk who called me up the other day and said he'd pay me thirty thousand dollars to go to bed with him?"

Richard opened an eye and looked at her. "No."

Connie didn't volunteer anything more than that. After a moment Richard opened the other eye and sat up. "Why didn't you tell me about this before?"

"I don't know. I guess I didn't really think much about it. He's a friend of my father and all talk. The guy is a real scumbag, you know?"

Richard grunted and sat back in his lounge.

Later, though, back in the condo, it was Richard who brought it up again. He was lying naked on the bed, sated, watching Connie as she brushed her hair.

"You know something, babe, maybe you ought to go to bed with him."

"Are you kidding?"

Richard sat up and swung his legs over the edge of the bed. "Why not? For thirty thousand dollars? All he wants to do is fuck you. I'd fuck him for that much. Hell, for thirty thousand, I'd kill him."

"Well, forget it. I'm not about to let that creep touch

me. I don't care how much money he has.''

Richard put a hand on her shoulder and turned her around to face him, wrapping an arm around her in a protective hug. "How about this, then? You tell him you're going to screw his brains out, but to make sure he lives up to his part of the deal, you want half the money up front. Then after he gives you the fifteen thousand, don't go through with it.''

"And he'll just forget about me ripping him off, huh? Won't bother me again, right? Sure!''

"Don't worry about him. If he gives you any trouble after we get his money, I'll take care of him. For good.''

Connie shuddered. Richard sounded . . . serious. She pulled away from him and said she didn't want to talk about it anymore. She wanted nothing to do with the idea.

They wouldn't discuss it any more. For a while.

52

"He called again today.'' Connie was trying not to blink, concentrating on keeping her hand steady while she applied eye makeup.

"At work?''

"Yes.''

"He has it bad for you.'' Richard sounded satisfied. Connie finished what she was doing and leaned away from the mirror. "He was bragging about the bundle of money he won in Las Vegas."

"When was he in Vegas?" asked Anderson.

"Oh, he's still there. He said he'll be back on Saturday. He wants me to meet him at Davis Brothers Cafeteria in Bartow. Said they have a broiled shrimp special there that he likes."

"And . . . ?"

"I told him I couldn't make it."

"What the hell did you do that for?"

"You know. . . ."

"Okay, drop it."

They did. Later, though, at the kitchen table after supper, Richard brought a ray of hope to Connie's heart by voluntarily bringing up the subject of marriage. Usually she was the one to initiate any conversation about that; though if she wanted to talk about the idea of maybe setting a date, he generally wanted to delay anything so specific. But this evening Richard was the first to mention the idea.

"You really want to?" she asked.

"You know I do. There's only one thing keeping me from making it official. You know?"

"Really?"

"That's money, babe. You know how hard it is. I got the mortgage on the place here and the car payments. And it's gonna be rough adding a wife and two kids on top of everything else. Not that I don't want to do it, mind. I really do. But it won't be easy. If we had a little money to get started on, I think it would work out good."

Connie was overjoyed. They spent much of the evening talking about the future.

Later, in bed, Richard asked, "Do you think Grantham is going to call you again?"

"I guess so. Why?"

"If he asks you out again, say yes."

"How come?"

"Because you'll go to dinner with him and then when the two of you come back out to the parking lot, I'll slip up and rob him. If he's as good at gambling as he keeps telling you he is, he ought to be loaded. I'll take every blessed cent he has." He snapped his fingers. "You know, the best place to do it would be the Sabal Point Holiday Inn. Yeah."

Richard was not joking. Connie was now convinced of that. The question was, did she want to go along with him and be able to get the money so they could get married? Or did she want to risk losing him? If she wanted to keep Richard—to marry him—she had to do what he wanted.

And anyway, Bob Grantham was just what she'd told Richard he was—a scumbag. Moreover, he could afford to lose a little money. He was rolling in the stuff. He told her so himself—and he was going to get more in some kind of settlement. The guy was such a creep. He *deserved* to get robbed.

"Okay."

"What?"

"I said, okay. We'll do . . . whatever."

Richard smiled.

53

Connie was alarmed when she received a call the next day, Thursday, at Remsgar. It was Bob Grantham and he said he was calling from *Houston*!

He was on his way back right then and would be flying in to Orlando that afternoon, not on Saturday like she'd discussed with Richard. Now what was she supposed to do?

Feeling her way carefully into the conversation, she asked Grantham if he needed a ride home from the airport. He told her no, he had his car there.

But, predictably, Lyin' Bob Grantham had one thing first and foremost in his thoughts.

He did not need a ride, he told her, but he sure would be pleased if she met him at the airport and followed him to a motel for some Welcome Home loving.

Connie wasn't sure what Richard would want her to do. But she knew Richard would not want her to let Grantham and his money completely off the hook. The best thing, she decided, would be to set something up with Grantham now and then talk to Richard to see what he wanted her to do next.

Trembling, she told Grantham she would be at the airport to meet him.

Grantham was quick to give her his flight number. He sounded awfully pleased.

As soon as she disconnected from Grantham she put in a call to Richard's pager. In a matter of minutes he got back with her.

"Take the rest of today off. Tell them you're sick or whatever, but get off. I'll meet you at the shopping center across the road in half an hour."

"Across the road from here?"

"Yeah. Half an hour."

Richard was already there waiting for her when Connie pulled up in the silver Pontiac Fiero that the dealership gave her to drive. He was carrying a brown sports bag when he got out of the Buick that Connie had sold him. Telling Connie to get into the passenger seat, Richard got behind the wheel and put his bag on the floorboard in front of her. He put the car in gear and headed out of town.

Once they were on Interstate 4 en route to Orlando, he told her to look in the bag. Connie bent over and unzipped it. Inside was a revolver with a long barrel. She quickly closed the bag again.

Richard had come up with an alternate plan that he explained to Connie while they drove. They would go into the terminal together, but once inside they would separate. Connie was to meet Grantham at the gate and accompany him to his car. Richard would tail them at a slight distance. Once Grantham reached his car, Richard would come up from behind and hit him over the head. He would take the money and walk away. Very simple. Practically foolproof.

Connie sat quietly and listened while the flat terrain rushed past her car window. Every moment took her nearer to the confrontation between her lover and the man who thought he was about to become her lover.

54

The TranStar flight was right on time, and Bob Grantham seemed pleased to see her as an attendant with a wheelchair brought him out of the umbilical ramp to the terminal building. He tried to kiss her, but Connie turned her head as if by accident so as to deflect the kiss at the last moment. He wound up kissing her cheek instead, and even at that Connie cringed.

Over Grantham's shoulder she could see Richard sitting in a nearby waiting area. He saw but did not seem to respond to her difficulty with this grabby, ugly old man, who was old enough to be her father.

A skycap brought a wheelchair for Grantham's use, and Bob began telling her about his trip.

"Where'd you park your car?"

"I caught a ride with a girlfriend." She managed a smile. "I guess I'll just have to depend on you for a ride from here."

Grantham positively beamed, happy to mistake Connie's intentions for the rest of the day—and night.

They collected Grantham's luggage and caught a shuttle to the long-term parking lot where he had left his car. There was no sign of Richard now. Either he was so very good at following someone that even Connie could not spot him, or he had somehow lost contact.

They reached Grantham's Thunderbird and he helped Connie into the passenger seat. He deposited his flight bag in the trunk of the car and hung a garment bag on a window hook.

There was no sign of Richard Anderson or of Connie's little Fiero when Grantham pulled out of the airport parking lot.

Connie became all the more alarmed when Grantham, instead of driving onto the Interstate that would take them back to Polk County, headed onto South Orange Blossom Trail.

"Where are we going?"

Grantham smiled. "Don't worry. I have to make a quick stop before we head home. It won't take long."

Orlando's Trail district is sleazy, with topless bars, adult book stores, and other venues of the flesh trade. It was into this garishly lighted strip that Grantham now took her. She was truly confused when he pulled into the lot outside a place called Flashdancer, which advertised exotic dancers and near nudity.

"Want to go in with me?" Grantham offered as if that were the most normal thing possible.

"No. I'll wait in the car. Just hurry."

It was at least twenty minutes before Grantham concluded whatever business it was that he had at Flashdancer and came back outside. From there he drove to a convenience market, where he bought a beer for himself and a bottle of Riunite wine for Connie. She gratefully twisted the cap off and began sipping the chilled lambrusco straight from the bottle. It seemed to help calm her down.

One thing she did not have to worry about was conversation. Grantham was entirely capable of supplying conversation sufficient for both of them. While he drove he told her all about Las Vegas, in particular about all the hookers he met while he was there.

"You know what? I'm hungry," he said at one point.

It was an opening and she took it, reverting to the original plan she and Richard had agreed upon. "You know, Mr. Grantham—I mean, Bob—there's a real nice restaurant in Tampa. At the Sabal Park Holiday Inn."

"No way. I just spent the day in the air, and I'm tired. I thought maybe we could get a bite to eat on our way back to my place. We'll be in Winter Haven soon, and that's when you start earning your money, honey."

This wasn't going at all the way it was supposed to. Richard didn't have any idea where Grantham lived, and she still couldn't see the Fiero behind them.

"That can wait. What I really need to get me in the mood is a good meal at a nice place with atmosphere. I like the Holiday Inn at Sabal Park."

"Are you serious? A Holiday Inn?"

"Yeah." She sweetened the suggestion just a little by leaning over and giving his arm a little squeeze.

"Okay. Whatever you want, darling."

Connie felt a lot better once the Winter Haven exit was safely behind them and the Thunderbird was headed for Tampa. But if Richard wasn't at the Holiday Inn, what was she going to do? She hoped she wouldn't have to actually sleep with Grantham while she was waiting for Richard to show up.

And if she did . . . jeez, this was lousy.

What she hoped was that Richard would be there waiting for them at the Holiday Inn and rob Grantham like they'd intended to start with. Then everything would be all right.

55

"Let's go in the lounge and have a drink first, okay?"

"Look, I'm tired and I'm hungry, and I got big plans for after, so let's go ahead and eat."

"You know, a drink first makes me horny. So can't we stop at the lounge first? Please?"

It somehow worked. Connie couldn't believe Grantham was letting himself be led around as he was; but he was. And a good thing, too, because there was no sign of Richard in the restaurant, and what she wanted to do was hold Grantham at bay until Richard showed up, from wherever he was.

Grantham was unenthusiastic about the beer he ordered, but Connie practically quivered with pleasure over her drink. She also excused herself to go to the bathroom and made a beeline for a pay phone.

She dialed Richard's pager and punched in the number of the public telephone on the wall. She waited several minutes without a response and eventually had to go back to the bar where Grantham was waiting. She gave him a smile and ordered another drink.

Unable to postpone it any longer, they went into the restaurant and had a leisurely dinner.

"You know," Grantham said at one point, "I'm fifty-one years old. But I'll be fifty-two tomorrow. Did you know that?'' He grinned and reached for her knee. ''When I think about the gift you're gonna give me later on, why, I feel like I'm celebrating early.''

''I've been thinking about that, Bob. And I have this friend who has a place not far from here. It would be just perfect for us to . . . you know.''

''Let's go.''

''Can't we have another drink before we leave? Please?''

''No. Let's get out of here.''

There still was no sign of Richard. Connie's only hope at this point was that Richard had gone home when he lost them at the airport.

They reached Anderson's condo about 8:30, and Connie used her key to let them in. Grantham did not even bother to take off the baseball cap he was wearing. He was in a state of arousal before he even reached for her.

''I'll be right back.'' Connie twisted away from Grantham and ran up the stairs hoping to find Richard there.

The unit was empty—except for herself and Bob Grantham.

56

Prosecutor John Skye rubbed the shelf of his jaw beneath his right ear, turned and looked at the jury while he asked Connie Beasley to continue her account of the night of May 7.

"I went back downstairs. I offered Mr. Grantham a drink, either liquor, tea, or whatever he wanted, and he said tea was fine, so I went in and fixed some. I turned on the TV, and we drank the tea. Mr. Grantham was sitting on the left side of the couch and I was sitting in a recliner that was next to it."

"Okay. What happened between you and Mr. Grantham?"

"We were talking. He talked about the hookers and how he wanted to go ahead and go to bed. That's all he had on his mind—sex. That's what he thought he was going to get.

"And I put him off and told him we had all night. That my friend was going to be gone and there was no sense in rushing things. And he was getting a little antsy, but he calmed down, and he was just sitting there with the TV on."

"Did you ever go to the bathroom?"

"Yes, sir."

"Where?"

"The downstairs bathroom."

"How long were you in there?"

"I was probably in there about eight minutes because I was trying to stall for time."

"What happened when you came back out?"

"Mr. Grantham was still on the couch, and I went back to sitting in the recliner."

"Was there a telephone in the living room where he was sitting?"

"Yes, there was."

There was no way Connie could have known it or testified to it, but it was while she was in the bathroom stalling for more time that Grantham, presumably bored with the inattention and wanting time to pass more quickly, placed the call to Rudy Benton, that later proved to be so important in the discovery of Beasley and of Richard Anderson.

"What happened next?"

"The next thing that happened was the door flew open and Richard came in."

57

Bob Grantham tried to jump to his feet but could not because of his disability.

Connie was stunned into immobility for another reason. Richard looked ridiculous. He seemed to be in disguise, which consisted of a silly pair of narrow-lensed glasses and a Band-Aid on his left cheek. Connie thought it had to be about the dumbest excuse for a disguise she'd ever seen. And the most useless right from the get-go because Grantham had never seen or heard of Richard Anderson before. There was no need for any sort of disguise, much less this silly getup.

Still, he was here now and she was grateful for that. She was, in fact, so grateful for not having to sleep with Grantham that it was only much, much later that it occurred to her that by bringing Grantham to Richard's condo she had pretty much sealed the old lecher's fate. There was no way Richard could rob him now without killing him, since Grantham would be able to escort the cops back to the condo afterward. In a parking lot sure, but not here. Even if she had thought about that at the time, though, it was already too late.

Taken aback by the stupid disguise attempt, Connie had to scramble to keep up with the equally silly dialogue Richard was coming up with without plan or warning.

"Oh hi, Connie. You'll have to excuse me. I guess I should have knocked. I didn't know you had company. Is Joyce back yet?"

Joyce? Who the hell was Joyce? Connie shook her head. Joyce. Ah, the girlfriend from whom she'd borrowed the condo—that would work. And Richard seemed to be playing at a missing girlfriend's boyfriend, or something. The whole thing was really quite weird.

Not to Richard. He shut the door behind him and came on into the living room. "I guess the reason you're here is to get your car back. Here you go." He tossed Connie's car keys to her.

By now Grantham was recovering from his surprise. Loudly he demanded, "Who the hell are you, and what are you doing with my girl's car?"

Richard gave Grantham a dirty look. "Who the hell am I? Well, who the fuck are you?" Before Grantham could answer Richard plunged ahead, opting for a quick offensive instead of giving Grantham time to put him into a defensive posture. "I'll tell you who the hell I am. This is my girlfriend's place, and her friend here"— he pointed at Connie—"lent me her car. Is that okay with you, man?"

Grantham glared at the younger man but said nothing.

Turning to Connie, Richard said, "It looks like Joyce is going to be late getting home, huh?"

"More like tomorrow," Connie said, finally picking up on the ploy. "She let me have the apartment for the night."

Richard began pacing the living room, ranting loudly about being stranded now without a car and needing a ride home. He made that point loud and clear. His own car was somewhere else and he needed a ride home somehow. The implication was clear. If Bob Grantham expected to have any time alone with Connie this night, he first would have to drive this madman home.

The thing Connie's eyes kept being drawn to no matter how hard she concentrated on looking away was the item that Richard was carrying in his right hand.

It was the zippered satchel she had looked into earlier—with the gun inside.

58

As they walked outside Richard hung back and let Grantham take the lead. Connie dropped a little behind Grantham, too. Richard silently mouthed "You drive."

Connie shook her head and silently mouthed "No."

The look Richard gave her was ugly, but aloud he said, "Will you ride in front with your friend?" He got into the backseat of Grantham's Thunderbird, and Connie got into the front passenger side seat.

With Richard directing the way, and Grantham at the wheel, they pulled out onto 56th Street and then took a left onto Sligh Avenue, then to US 301, where they turned right.

Connie sat half-turned in the front seat so that she could see a very unhappy looking Bob Grantham and at the same time keep an eye on Richard.

Grantham kept glancing into the rearview mirror, sending daggers at Anderson in the backseat. He was unable to see what Richard was doing at lap level, though, but Connie could. Richard took a pair of black gloves out of his satchel—they were shiny and probably leather but it was dark and she couldn't tell for sure about that—and began very methodically pulling them on, smoothing and adjusting each finger so that everything felt just right.

And once the gloves were on and she looked back again, Richard was holding a gun. It was not the same gun she'd seen in the satchel earlier. This one was smaller and a different color than that one had been, but it was a gun—that much she was sure of. She felt a thrill of excitement rush through her.

They were going to do this. They were really going to do this.

"This is where I live. Turn in here."

Grantham slowed and pulled into a building complex called Breckenridge.

"No, this isn't it. Make a U-turn."

Grantham slowed and made the sharp turn, then hit his brakes sharply and almost, but not quite, stopped; the car was left at an idle so that it was rolling at a walking pace virtually on its own.

Grantham, angry and wanting to protest, said, "What the—"

A shot rang out, very loud within the close confines of the Thunderbird. Then three more in rapid succession.

Connie choked back an impulse to scream—and scream and scream some more.

59

Richard Anderson slouched low in his chair at the defense table, shaking his head.

Prosecutor Skye ignored the display and asked his prize witness, "How many shots did you hear?"

"Four."

"In what succession?"

"He shot him once. It went bang. And then one, two, three right after that."

"What happened then?"

Even after so much time had lapsed, Connie became quite visibly pale, her cheeks drained of all color, and her forehead a stark, sickly white.

"Mr. Grantham fell into my lap." Her voice was small.

"Was he bleeding?"

"He was bleeding a lot. It was going in my skirt. I could feel it going down my legs."

60

"What the—"

Grantham was turning to look at Richard Anderson in the backseat of Grantham's Thunderbird. He had time enough to see the muzzle of the .22 automatic aimed pointblank at his forehead.

Time enough, too, to see the sheet of yellow flame that burst like a terrible blossom from the gun, illuminating the interior of the car like a flash of sudden lightning. It is problematic whether he had time enough to hear the thunderclap of the gunshot as well.

Alive then, or perhaps already dead from the tiny pellet of superheated lead that penetrated his brain, Robert Grantham remained upright seconds longer, his eyes fixed in the direction of the man who murdered him.

Anderson fired quickly again—one, two, three times more.

It was then that Grantham toppled sideways into Connie Beasley's lap, the blood pouring from his head and onto her skirt and his weight pinning her to the seat while hot blood saturated the cloth of her skirt and began to flow over the bare skin of her thighs.

When he fell over, Grantham's hand dropped away from the gearshift lever where he had been about to put the transmission into PARK, and his foot slipped off the brake pedal.

The car, still in gear and with the wheel cranked hard to the left after the abrupt U-turn, began slowly to roll without guidance.

Connie sat stunned, staring down at the dead man in her lap.

Richard was screaming at her, shouting for her to stop the car.

Connie tried. She really did. She tried to reach out with the toe of her left foot to reach the brake. Yet Grantham's dead weight kept her pinned in place. She could not move to reach the pedal. Connie was sobbing, and Richard was shouting angrily at her, and the car was rolling into a circle on its own.

Finally, desperately, Connie lurched to the side, forcing her weight against that of Robert Grantham's body. She managed to grab the tip end of the gear shift lever and shove it into PARK. The car rocked to a jolting stop.

Connie felt blank, empty. She couldn't think, couldn't comprehend, couldn't cope. She didn't *want* to have to cope with anything just then. It was all much too much.

The only thing she could think of was that at least it was quiet. Richard wasn't shouting at her any longer, and she was glad about that.

But the blood—she could feel the blood. It was so warm, and sticky. It made her skirt cling to her flesh like it had been when she was a tiny wee little girl and wet herself. The feeling was more than uncomfortable, it was shameful. She wanted to cry but knew she shouldn't. That would only make Richard mad, and she did not want Richard to be mad at her. She sat where she was, silent and rigid, and trembled with the fear that flushed and flowed through her body.

Richard leaned forward from behind the driver's seat and got the door open. He got out on that side of the car and came around and opened Connie's door. He took her by the arm and yanked her out from under Grantham's body.

Connie gaped in horror as a rush of blood spilled onto the seat where she had just been. The baseball cap he had been wearing fell off his head and tumbled onto the floor.

"Get in the back."

Connie nodded mutely and did as she was told. Then Richard took hold of Grantham's shirt and dragged the body half out of the car so the legs were clear of the driver's seat, then pushed the torso upright in the passenger seat.

Richard closed the passenger side door, making sure it was securely latched, then walked around and got behind the wheel. The engine was still running. He turned and looked at Connie and grinned.

"Killing somebody, babe. That's the ultimate high. You know?"

Connie shuddered.

Richard seemed not to notice. Still grinning he broke into laughter. Then he said, "Well, it took a sick son of a bitch to shoot someone four times, because the first time I shot him he was probably dead. But I shot him three more times."

Richard's laughter died, and he gave Connie a hard look. "Keep your mouth shut now and don't say a word. Not one."

Connie nodded and kept her mouth shut. Richard still had the gun in his hand, and a dead man on the seat beside him. It would take only a squeeze of his finger and there could be two dead people in the car with him. And his mood right now seemed crazy. It was like he really was high. Connie looked blindly out the car window. She had no idea what was beyond the glass, for the focus of her horror was all inside the car with her.

61

John Skye slowly and with painstaking thoroughness led Connie through the events of that night. Through every street and turn she could remember as Richard Anderson drove them through the dark streets of northeast Tampa, heading out Buffalo Avenue and jogging in and out of different neighborhoods as he searched for a place that would be to his liking, a place where he could dump the body that was slumped in the seat at his right side.

Finally, not far past the Holiday Inn where a few hours earlier Robert Grantham had eaten his last meal, Anderson pulled off the road.

"When we first turned in to make the left, he floorboarded it, and I remember my head hitting the top of the car. And I could hear the brush that was underneath the car—grass or whatever it was. I could hear brush hitting it. And he pulled in real fast and stopped and got out of the car and came around to the passenger's side and pulled Mr. Grantham out."

"Okay, what happened then? What did you do?"

"I was just sitting there. I was watching. I could see him out there. And then he realized he left the headlights on, and he came back and shut them off and went back."

"When you say he went back, where did he go?" Skye asked.

"He went back to put Mr. Grantham on a pile of sand."

"Tell us about where he pulled him."

"He put him on a pile of sand. I could see the sand. It was like a mound of dirt. From the floor it was probably about that high." She reached forward with the flat of her hand extended to show the height.

"You're indicating about four feet?" Skye asked.

"About four to five feet. And he pulled him up onto the sand and was straddling him. And he kept looking back at me. Finally he came back to the car and got the clothes bag Mr. Grantham had in the car and threw it out there somewhere near where the body was."

"When he returned to the car, did you see the body anymore?"

"No."

Skye wanted the jurors to be very clear on the next point, lest Anderson's defense team try to create a smokescreen later. "From the time of the shots, up until what you've just described, what sounds did you hear Mr. Grantham make?"

"I didn't hear him make any sounds."

"Breathing even?"

"No, sir."

"Did you see him move at all?"

"No, sir."

Once he was finished with that subject, John Skye looked at the jury while he asked Connie Beasley, "What was said between you and the defendant when he got back into the car?"

"He was always talking about me going to church and taking my children and he didn't go. And he said, 'You better thank your God that you kept your mouth shut, because I was thinking the whole time I was up there how I may have to kill you, too.' " Connie's voice was very small again, and her eyes darted sharply to the side, in the direction where Richard Anderson was seated, but stopping short each time so that she did not quite look directly at him.

"What happened then?"

"We went back to the apartment."

"Did Mr. Anderson say anything about the body on the way back to the apartment?"

"He said, 'You know, we should just come back here tonight and take the body and move it to Orlando so they'll think that somebody there did it.' "

"Did you ever do that?"

"No."

62

When they reached Richard's condo and went inside, Richard reached for her. Whether he wanted to talk, to have sex, to . . . whatever, she didn't know and didn't care. She twisted away from his grasp and fled up the stairs.

Every step of the way she was conscious of the heavy, sticky, horrid sensation of that dead man's wet blood on her skirt and drying on the skin of her legs.

She stripped off her clothes and turned the shower on. The hot, steaming water and the soap and the scrubbing, however, could not wash away the memory of the way the blood felt. She was afraid that sensation would be with her forever. She scrubbed and scrubbed and scrubbed.

When finally she came out again she found Richard downstairs. He must have gone out while she was in the shower, because he had Grantham's flight bag, the one Connie had seen Bob Grantham (God, was he really dead? Was all this really true?) put into the trunk of his car when they were at the airport. This afternoon that had been. That seemed impossible. Surely so much could not possibly have happened just since this afternoon.

As Connie watched, Anderson pulled several thin sheaves of currency from the flight bag, counted them and in disgust pitched them onto the glass-top coffee table in the living room.

"I can't believe I just fucking killed somebody for only twenty-six hundred dollars," Richard complained.

Connie didn't know whether he wanted her to sympathize or complain along with him. She kept her mouth shut. It seemed the sensible thing to do.

Richard told her to get her dress and anything else that had blood on it and bring everything downstairs. While she was doing that, he found a plastic garbage bag in which he placed Grantham's flight bag. Connie added her clothes, purse, and shoes. All were smeared with the clotted, drying blood.

Then, with Richard driving the Thunderbird and Connie following close behind in her little Pontiac, they took a seemingly random drive through Tampa, ending up eventually at the airport, where they entered by way of an unattended ticket vending machine.

She noticed every now and then when light from a street lamp or a passing car momentarily illuminated the interior of the Thunderbird that even while they drove Richard was busy wiping and scrubbing at the seat of the Thunderbird as if to mop up all the blood Grantham had spilled there.

He wiped and scraped some more after he parked in the Tampa International lot. Connie waited nearby in her

Fiero. Finally satisfied, or at least resigned that he could not do anything more, Richard laid a newspaper across the seat and joined Connie.

From there they went back to Richard's condo, where he showered and changed clothes.

He put his bloody clothing into the garbage bag with the other things and disposed of it simply by walking across the road and tossing the bag into a dumpster.

Then, in Connie's car but with Richard driving, they went down the street a quarter mile or so to a bridge spanning the slow-moving Hillsborough River.

He checked the rearview mirror, then stopped in the middle of the bridge. He opened the car door and leaned halfway out and, like a basketball player making a hook shot, tossed the .22 automatic and its magazine separately into the river. Connie heard the distinct splashes as they hit the water.

Richard drove to the end of the bridge, turned around, and came back to stop again, this time disposing of the black gloves he had worn when he shot Grantham.

Richard was hungry when they returned to the condo again. Connie had no appetite. She did, however, enjoy the closeness with him later when they finally went to bed. They made love before dropping off to sleep.

63

Richard left early the next morning. Connie assumed he was going to work. She herself slept in late because she did not have to be on the showroom floor until one. Richard called about nine to see how she was. That was thoughtful of him, she thought, assuring him that she was fine and would see him later.

She spent a lazy, unhurried morning at Richard's place, and left a little early so that she could stop at J. C. Penney's to look for some shoes. She'd had to throw her only nice pair away the night before because they had blood on them, and she wanted to replace them.

As she was driving away from the condo, though, she saw Richard's car approaching. He motioned for her to stop, so she did.

He wanted her to see something in the trunk of his car.

Connie thought she was doing okay. Now she began trembling again. The thing in the trunk of Richard's car looked like a real machine gun.

"Where'd you get that?" she whispered.

"Friend of mine owed me a favor."

"But . . ."

"If the heat's ever on, babe, I can take some people out with that."

"Where are you taking it?"

He gave her an odd look. "Home. Where else?"

"I have to go, Richard." She got into her Fiero and drove to J. C. Penney's, but her thoughts were not solely on shoes now.

Connie knew that she did not want to go home just yet and face her parents. So she called them from work to say she was staying over with Richard again that night. Her mother told her the children were fine and to go ahead.

When later she got to the condo, though, Richard was not there. She went to their favorite restaurant but couldn't find him, so she bought herself a sandwich to go and went back to the condo to wait for him.

Instead she received a telephone call. He was, he told her rather obliquely, some three or four hundred miles from Tampa—never mind where—and was calling to check on her.

He called again sometime in the wee hours of that night. This time he gave no reason for calling but said he was still in the same place as before.

Nervous and more than a little bit worried, Connie became frightened staying alone in Richard's place. Wrapped in a light afghan that she'd been dozing under on Richard's couch, she went next door and asked neighbor Sal Lodato if she could spend the rest of the night at his place where there would be other people around. It was four o'clock in the morning, and Connie was scared.

Lodato let her sleep on his daughter's bed because his daughter was away for the night, and at seven o'clock the next morning, he awakened Connie so that she would be able to make it in to work on time.

She stopped at Richard's place to change out of the clothes she'd been sleeping in, and as soon as she walked in the door the telephone began ringing.

It was Richard, and he was furious.

Apparently he had been calling her through the night,

and the longer time stretched with the telephone going unanswered the angrier he became. He was even more upset when she told him where she had been. He found it embarrassing that she would have gone to the neighbors for help.

That night, when Connie returned to the condo after work, the place was still empty. Richard finally did show up late in the evening. He said nothing about where he had been or why—and she did not think in terms of him moving Robert Grantham's body to another location where it would not be found—but he did complain about getting a speeding ticket on his way home.

Yet during those days, and in the days to come, the intensity of the affair between Connie Beasley and Richard Anderson cooled.

She was still in love with him, she thought. But things were not really the same as they had been before they murdered and robbed Bob Grantham.

64

Richard Anderson was meat on a hook, waiting to be hauled into the cooler—unless the defense team could create doubt in the jurors' minds about Connie Beasley's testimony. Which was quite naturally the tack attorney William Fuente selected when Beasley was turned over for cross-examination.

First reiterating the background—Beasley's initial

meetings with Grantham, her relationship with Anderson, the fact that the two men never met—Fuente began homing in not on Connie Beasley's testimony before this jury but on the statements she had given earlier when questioned by Ray Velboom and Steve Davenport and, later, during her sworn testimony before a grand jury.

There were more than a few inconsistencies among those several versions.

The first version, given to the FDLE agents shortly after her arrest, could be graded A for drama but only about a D for originality. In it Connie said Richard was very upset and protective of her when he learned that Grantham was making suggestive telephone calls. The next time Grantham called asking to date her, she gave him Richard's address and said she would meet him there. Her intention, she told the agents, was to bring the two men together so that Richard could have a talk with Grantham and dissuade the older man from sexually harassing Connie.

In that version tragedy struck because Richard was not at home when Grantham arrived. Connie said she tried to fight Grantham off but that the man attacked her and ripped her clothing and was attempting to forcibly rape her when Richard came home and, leaping to her rescue, grabbed Grantham and hauled him outside. Connie said she never saw Grantham again after that.

Fuente made sure the jury was getting the full impact of this patently self-serving statement.

Then he fired his second salvo.

Did Ms. Beasley remember a statement she had made to the FDLE agents at a later date amending her first statement?

Well, yes, as a matter of fact she did. This time her basic story was unchanged. Once again Richard came to her rescue when he returned home to find Robert Grantham in the act of raping the innocent Ms. Beasley. But this time Connie admitted that she went along when

Richard took Grantham out and, yes, she was there when Grantham was killed.

"And you were given an opportunity by those FDLE agents to talk to them, tell them the truth?" Fuente asked.

"Yes, sir."

"Did you tell them the truth?"

Connie's voice was low and halting. "No, I did not."

"Did you lie?"

"I lied, yes, sir."

Still, the basic fact in all the versions as alleged by Connie Beasley was that Richard Anderson did the actual killing. And if he wanted to secure an acquittal for his client, Fuente had to find some way to shake the jury's confidence in *any* story put forward by Beasley.

"Do you appreciate the seriousness of being under oath and testifying?"

"Yes, sir."

"And you've told the truth here today?"

"Yes, sir."

"Do you know what it means to lie under oath?"

"Yes, I do."

"And you're telling the jury that you have not committed perjury today?"

Beasley looked him square in the eye and said, "No, I have not."

William Fuente turned away from Beasley and looked slowly from one juror to another. Then, glancing back in Beasley's general direction, he offhandedly asked, "Have you ever perjured yourself?"

Connie sat mutely in the witness box. As her silence lengthened the jurors began looking from her to Fuente and back again, waiting for one of them to say something. Finally, William Fuente spoke. "Did you appear and testify before the grand jury on July 15?"

Connie knew what was coming, and there was no

place for her to hide. "Yes." Her voice was scarcely audible.

"And even though you were sworn to tell the truth you lied, didn't you?"

Connie again looked straight into Fuente's eyes, but this time she did not seem so confident in her response. "Yes."

"Under oath?"

"Yes."

"That is perjury, is it not?"

"I guess so."

"So you have no qualms about lying under oath, do you?"

Connie squared her shoulders and lifted her chin. "Sir, I have not lied today."

"Why did you lie in the previous statements you made to the FDLE agents and the grand jury?"

"I was scared."

"About what?"

"I don't know."

"Well, let me ask you, were you concerned about the welfare of Richard Anderson when you first talked to the police?"

She hesitated, then said, "Probably not. I was worried about myself."

"In fact, you were trying to lay this on Richard Anderson, weren't you?"

She did not answer the question.

Not willing to let it go at that, Fuente gave her an accusatory look and again asked, "Weren't you trying to lay it on Richard Anderson and take it off Connie Beasley?"

"Yeah, maybe I was. I didn't admit my guilt. You're right. I was scared."

"Scared about going to prison? Scared about losing your children?"

"Yes."

"So what you did was downplay your involvement and instead blamed it totally on Richard Anderson?"

"Yes."

"Are you protecting yourself today, Ms. Beasley?"

This time she had her answer ready for him. "No. I'm not protecting myself. As you know, I'm probably going to prison, too. I have no reason to lie. I'm telling the truth."

"No reason to lie?" Fuente's voice was heavy with sarcasm. "Do you know what the penalty is for first-degree murder?"

"I know there are several different penalties, but I don't know exactly."

"Did you think that maybe one could be put to death for murder?"

"Sure. Everyone knows that."

"And didn't you meet on July 24 with Mr. Skye and reach an agreement between yourself and the State Attorney's office?"

"Yes."

"And in return for your testifying here today, you were allowed to plead guilty to third-degree murder and face a maximum of three years in prison, correct?"

"Yes."

"So it is quite possible that you could be placed on probation and not even serve any prison time. Right?"

"That will be up to the judge to decide."

"But it could happen?"

"It could."

William Fuente turned away, paused for a moment and turned back to face her again. "I believe there is one thing we can agree on, and that is you did not admit your part in the crime until after you were promised no more than three years."

"Yes, sir."

"So in effect you are still protecting yourself, aren't you, Ms. Beasley?"

Fuente knew how to leave a strong impression with the jurors. Before Beasley had time to answer that last dart, the defense attorney abruptly turned away from her and went back to the defense table. "I have no further questions of this witness."

Reasonable doubt—a reasoned doubt. That was all Fuente needed. And surely the testimony of an admitted perjurer could reasonably be doubted.

65

Ray Velboom's and Steve Davenport's work had not ended with the arrests of Richard Anderson and Connie Beasley. Anything but. And it was during the trial that the results of these extra efforts became apparent.

The prosecution had a great deal of blood to work with. The interior of Grantham's Thunderbird was coated with it—all of it Type A. But what blood type had Grantham been?

Hospital records were blank on that critical subject, as they long ago learned.

It was Davenport who came up with a long-shot possibility to resolve that question.

Robert Grantham was a man who had drifted from job to job in the past. He was a gambler and possibly much worse. Davenport's idea was that at some point during this irregular and often rocky journey, Bob Grantham must have been broke.

And what does a down-and-out would-be sharpie like Bob Grantham do when he needs a few dollars to parlay into his next fortune? Very often, Davenport knew, he sells his blood.

Somewhere between Tampa and Orlando there was at least a chance that Grantham may have sold a pint or two of his best.

Davenport's idea paid dividends when he checked with a blood and plasma laboratory in Lakeland, just a few miles from Grantham's hometown of Winter Haven.

Accordingly, John Skye was able to put Brenda Bradley on the witness stand. A technician at Sera-Tec Biologicals, Bradley's job was to take the temperatures and blood pressures of potential donors, then take a small, fingertip blood sample and apply standard tests to determine that person's blood type.

The test is really quite simple. Small samples are put onto two sides of a glass slide and different clotting agents are added on each side. If the blood clots on one side it is Type A, on the other side Type B, and if no clotting occurs on either side then it is Type O.

"Do you record it [on an individual's chart] the same day as you do the test?" Skye asked his witness.

"Yes."

At which point William Fuente raised a technical argument before the court. Outside the presence of the jury he was allowed to ask Ms. Bradley, "Do you have an independent recollection of drawing a particular blood sample from a particular person on a particular day, specifically the one you are here for today?"

"No."

Fuente asked Judge Graybill to reject Sera-Tec's chart on Robert Grantham as inadmissible. The judge overruled the defense objection and allowed Bradley to testify.

According to the Sera-Tec records, Robert T. Grantham of Winter Haven, Florida, had Type A blood. This was the same as was found inside his Thunderbird in such immense quantity the previous May. The finding did not show that the blood in the car *was* Grantham's— but it could have been.

Skye decided also to give the jurors fingerprint testimony in order to insure the jury members would not think he was trying to hide something that did not fit with the facts of the case.

In fact, there was nothing to hide.

Exhaustive crime-scene work on both Grantham's car and Anderson's condominium unit turned up plenty of fingerprints, and Skye had each one of them described for the jurors.

The unfortunate part of it was that the technicians found plenty of Richard Anderson's prints in the condo and dozens of Robert Grantham's in the car. But there were none of Anderson's in the car nor any of Grantham's in the condo. And Connie Beasley did not show up in any of the fingerprinting anywhere.

Still, it was this sort of thoroughness that is required to make sure every nuance and technicality is accounted for in a capital trial.

Slogging through the end of the fingerprint testimony with FDLE crime laboratory analyst Ed Guenther, Skye asked, "Now, how many latents were lifted from the vehicle?"

"I believe twenty-four."

"Of those twenty-four, how many were you able to identify as belonging to Mr. Grantham?"

"Thirteen."

"Which means there are ten or so that are unidentifiable?"

"Yes."

"And they can be anybody's?"

"Yes, they could."

"Now, were you able to lift any latent fingerprints from the firearm given to you for inspection?"

"No. It is highly unlikely that a print would be developed off a gun after it's been in water."

66

When Connie Beasley was interviewed by FDLE agents following her arrest, she was sure she remembered exactly where Richard Anderson stopped when he threw the murder weapon into the Hillsborough River.

It therefore should have been a simple enough thing to recover the gun. Just go to that spot, look into the water, and there it surely must be.

Except the agents knew going in that it would not be anything like that easy.

The Hillsborough, like most of Florida's many rivers, flows slowly, ambling along at a leisurely pace due to Florida's nearly flat terrain, which necessitates a shallow rate of fall. Mountain streams are swift and noisy due to the steepness of the slopes they travel across. Florida's creeks, in contrast, are nearly all placid.

But the contrast does not stop there. Swift mountain streams normally carry water that is crystal clear; visible sediments are washed away in the fast-moving waters. Slow and gentle flows like the Hillsborough pick up all manner of discoloring agents, tannin in particular, as they dawdle along through cypress swamps and oak stands and pine barrens. The waters become turbid and opaque. Such streams in Florida are quite aptly called "blackwater" rivers.

The Hillsborough is a good example of the type. And anyone looking for anything on its bottom needs to be very good—and very lucky.

The agent in charge of the firearm recovery team was Rose Giansanti, working out of the Tampa office. She asked the Hillsborough County Sheriff's Office for the expert assistance of their underwater recovery team.

The dive team agreed to help and soon met Giansanti at the 56th Street bridge, beneath the spot where Connie Beasley said the gun was thrown.

The scuba divers had been in the Hillsborough before and knew what to expect. Between the blackwater effect and a glut of solid particulates, the Hillsborough is a nightmare for a search team.

Artificial light will not penetrate the silt, reflecting off it the way the high beams of an automobile will create a blinding effect in thick fog. The only sure search method available to the divers was to sift, by hand, through the muck on the bottom.

In order to conduct this painstaking search in an orderly fashion, the team members long ago worked out a simple but effective control technique.

Each selecting a support pillar to work from, the divers loaded their belts with lead and deflated their buoyancy compensators so they would be carried to the bottom without having to struggle to stay under. Once there, each diver attached a stout cord to the base of his assigned pillar.

Diver Kevin Johnson found the conditions as bad as he had expected. But like the others who were conducting the search, he knew what to do.

Once he had his attachment point, he paid out a few feet of line and slowly, carefully, began feeling his way

along the bottom of the river. By remaining at the end
of his tether—but not tied to it; if anything went wrong
it was not the river bottom he would want to be tied
to—his search pattern was quite naturally a semicircle,
like the sweep of a windshield wiper across a lumpy,
muddy, sometimes positively disgusting windshield.

At the end of each sweep Johnson paid out another
couple feet of line and turned back the other way.

It was slow work.

Above water, special agent Giansanti was becoming
worried. The divers had been down more than an hour.
She was afraid Beasley's information would not prove
correct.

At the bottom of the Hillsborough, Kevin Johnson
was thinking the same thing, at least so far as his search
area was concerned. He literally had come to the end of
his rope. He ran out of line and hovered in neutral buoyancy, watching his bubbles disappear while he thought
about admitting defeat and following the air stream to
the surface.

One more sweep, he decided.

He regretted that decision immediately. A sharp pain
shot through his left hand. Something sharp enough to
pierce his heavy diving glove was embedded in his finger. Taking a look, he discovered a fish hook sticking
out of his glove. And, more important, his finger. Hoping that the hook hadn't penetrated deep into his flesh,
he gritted his teeth—figuratively, that is; the mouthpiece
of his regulator prevented any serious clenching of his
teeth—and pulled the hook out. His finger began to
throb but seemed to have escaped serious injury.

About to resume his last sweep, Johnson saw
something out of the corner of his eye.

On the dark and muddy river bottom he saw a patch
of pale, clean sand.

And when he swam closer to it, he saw, not a foot

away from his mask, a chrome-plated .22-caliber semi-automatic handgun.

Johnson discovered that it is entirely possible to grin with a scuba regulator in one's mouth.

67

Prosecutor Skye handed Deputy Johnson a handgun and asked if he recognized it.

"Yes, this appears to be the automatic I found."

After explaining about the search under Skye's questions, Johnson said, "It was like the gun was waiting for me on a silver platter. I picked it up, surfaced, and called the other divers, who went back down and tried to find the magazine. They couldn't find it, though."

"What did you do with the gun?"

"I gave it to Agent Giansanti, who placed it in a bag of water."

"Why did she do that?"

"So it wouldn't rust before being processed by the lab," the deputy said.

After Johnson's testimony, crime lab analyst Ed Guenther was recalled. Still under oath, and with Skye providing the requisite questions, Guenther identified each of the four .22-caliber bullet casings that were found inside Robert Grantham's Thunderbird. Four casings to match the four shots that Connie Beasley said

Richard Anderson fired when he killed Grantham. Guenther was excused again.

The next witness was Joseph Hall, a firearms expert from the FDLE Tampa Regional Crime Laboratory. Lee Cannon took over from Skye to handle Hall's testimony.

Hall quickly identified the handgun in evidence as the same one SA Rose Giansanti gave him to test. He also went through the obligatory exercise of similarly identifying each of the four cartridge casings he had been given by Ed Guenther.

"What tests were conducted on these exhibits?" Cannon asked.

Hall said he first found a substitute magazine to replace the one missing from the gun he was testing. He then fired the gun into a bullet recovery tank.

Instead of the bullet, though, Hall's interest lay in the empty casings that were ejected by the gun after it fired. The freshly fired casings were examined under a microscope and then compared side by side with each of the casings found in Robert Grantham's automobile.

The markings left on the soft brass cartridge cases by the firing pin and ejection pawl were identical on both the test firing samples and the crime-scene evidence.

Since case markings are as unique and distinctive as fingerprints, Hall was able to conclude with certainty that the empty cartridges recovered from the Thunderbird had been fired by the exact gun recovered by Deputy Johnson.

Not done yet, however, Cannon pushed for a little more. He asked Hall in which direction cartridge casings are ejected from that particular make and model firearm.

"To the right," Hall answered.

"All right, sir, if the gun was fired inside a vehicle, would casings be found on the right hand side of the car?"

Fuente immediately entered an objection to the question, but Judge Graybill allowed the question to be posed.

"As I said, the pistol is designed to eject casings to the right, but I can't say specifically where each and every cartridge casing would wind up."

Satisfied, Cannon had no further questions of Hall.

The prosecution was not satisfied that the jury could not find a reason to doubt, though. The gun came from the river and had been fired inside the car. But just whose gun was it, anyway?

68

Ever since the Gun Control Act of 1968, whenever a firearm is sold by a licensed gun dealer a form is created listing the name and address of the purchaser. These forms are placed on file with the Bureau of Alcohol, Tobacco and Firearms (ATF).

While Joseph Hall was busy conducting laboratory tests on the gun in question, FDLE agent Rose Giansanti was equally busy tracing the ownership of the Jennings .22.

The first step toward that end was to make an inquiry with the ATF, where, checking the gun by manufacturer and serial number, ATF special agent Wayne Tucci was able to tell them that the gun was sold through Hancock Firearms, a dealer in Thomasville, Georgia. The ATF did not, however, have information on the purchaser.

Giansanti called Don Hancock, the Georgia gun dealer, who checked back through his records and found that he had sold the gun approximately two years earlier to a local Thomasville man named Albert Hurst.

Giansanti bucked the lead over to Ray Velboom, who in turn called on the Georgia Bureau of Investigation's Thomasville office for assistance. There, John White, GBI assistant special agent in charge, spoke with Albert Hurst.

White reported that Hurst only owned the .22 for two months or so before selling it to his father-in-law.

Disappointment turned to elation when White further reported that while Albert Hurst could not recall his father-in-law's address, the man's name was James Parker, and he worked at a forklift company in Tampa, Florida.

Velboom immediately checked with Tampa Forklift, where Richard Anderson had worked. No, they had no James Parker on the payroll. Instead, Parker was found at a company called Yale Forklift.

The news again turned good. Yes, Parker recalled buying the palm-sized .22 from his son-in-law around Thanksgiving of 1985. But he had sold it sometime in 1986 to a man whom he worked with named Ira Bruce Andrews.

Yet Andrews was no longer employed at Yale; nor did he still live at the address he had given when he did work there.

Ray Velboom asked Pete Monti, the same persistent analyst who first uncovered Richard Anderson's murderous past, to see if he could locate Andrews.

After trailing the man by way of automobile registrations, utilities hook-ups, and several other long-shot methods, Monti located Ira Bruce Andrews.

"My name is Ira Bruce Andrews," the witness told Lee Cannon.

"And were you ever employed at Yale Forklift here in Tampa?"

"Yes, I was. In eighty-five and eighty-six."

"Now, do you know Mr. James Parker?"

"Yes, sir, I do."

"And did you ever buy a firearm from Mr. Parker?"

"Yes, I did."

"When did you buy it?"

"Sometime in eighty-six."

Cannon showed Andrews the little Jennings that had been used to kill Robert Grantham. "Is this the one you bought?"

Andrews first looked at the serial number, then nodded. "Yes, it is."

"Now, how long did you own the firearm?"

"Approximately a week."

"What did you do with it?"

"I sold it."

"Who did you sell it to?"

Andrews pointed across the room to the tall, mustachioed man seated at the defense table. "Mr. Anderson. He used to work at Yale Forklift with me. Before he started working for Tampa Forklift."

"Thank you. No further questions."

69

An intimidating figure of a man, large and muscular, Kenneth Gallon sat in the courtroom and watched television; as did also the jurors, spectators, and other participants in the trial. John Skye was presenting into evidence the video tape of a newscast originally aired on July 8, 1987, following the arrest of Connie Beasley and Richard Anderson. The newscast first outlined the arrest and murder charges, then showed the hunt for Grantham's body in a wooded area, then showed finally a scene of searchers in a boat also looking for the corpse.

"Now, Mr. Gallon, have you ever seen this before?"

"Yes, sir."

"And what date did you see it?"

"July eighth, at five o'clock."

"And where were you?"

"In the Hillsborough County jail."

"And who was there with you?"

"Anderson."

"Richard Anderson?"

"Yes, sir."

"Anyone else?"

"Tony House and Bernard Walker."

"Was Mr. Anderson watching the television during the broadcast?"

"Yes, sir."

"And did you hear him say anything in respect to that broadcast?"

"Yes, sir."

"Explain to us what he said and at what point."

"When they showed Miss Beasley, he pointed his finger and said, 'Boom, bitch, you're dead.' "

Skye looked at the jurors as if to emphasize that comment, but he did not interrupt the witness.

"Then [the camera] turned around," Gallon said, "and showed the part where they were in a boat area and [Anderson] said, 'Yeah, motherfucker, stay right there, because if the body is there the alligators done got it by now.' And then they turned around and showed another part where the man was on a three-wheel motorcycle and Anderson said, 'Motherfucker, get out of that area. Get out of that area.' "

"Anything else?"

"Then it went off."

"What happened after that?"

"We went in the back and he asked me to kill Miss Beasley. He said he would pay me two or three thousand dollars to have her killed."

At that point Anderson shook his head and smiled as if hearing something so impossible and ludicrous that it was beyond belief.

"And were you personally going to do it?" Skye asked the witness.

"No, sir. I was supposed to have somebody else do it."

"What did you discuss?"

"She was out on bail. He told me where her house was and that she got a little side window to get in, and it would be no problem."

"What did you do?"

"I called a friend of mine, Kevin Fitzpatrick."

"Who is he?"

"He's a sergeant at the sheriff's office. I told him what Anderson said."

"What happened then?"

"The FDLE agents came to see me and I told them. They were going to set it up like one of them was the hit man and get Anderson to say something to them about killing Miss Beasley. But it never worked out. Anderson got suspicious about somebody in the cell squealing on him. He even got in a fight with Bernard Walker, thinking it was him."

When defense attorney Mark Ober took over the cross-examination, his task was to discredit Gallon. Ober's demeanor in court, unlike that of defender William Fuente, was aggressive to the point of sometimes seeming pushy.

"Mr. Gallon, you knew that Richard Anderson was a ticket for you, didn't you?"

"Sir?"

"You knew if you lied and told Fitzpatrick that you had some information he could help you."

"I wasn't lying. I told him the truth."

"What were you in jail for this time?"

Skye objected, but after discussion the judge ruled the question should be answered. Ober pressed forward. "On July twentieth, did you appear before Circuit Judge Susan Bucklew and plead guilty to eight counts of armed robbery and three counts of aggravated battery?"

"I pleaded 'no contest.' "

"And did you know that the maximum penalty for armed robbery was life in prison?"

"Yes, sir." Gallon seemed completely unruffled, even serene in his demeanor.

"Have you been sentenced yet?"

"No, sir."

"Your sentencing has been continued on numerous occasions, hasn't it?"

"Yes, sir."

"In other words, you're not to be sentenced until the conclusion of this case?"

"Yes, sir."

Ober leaned across the lectern and fixed Gallon with a glare. "And your sentence depends upon the discretion of the State Attorney's office, doesn't it?"

"What do you mean?"

"Isn't it true that you made a deal with the State Attorney's office in which you would receive no more than twenty-two years in prison, even though you were facing a life sentence?"

"Yes, sir."

"And if they decide that you cooperated here today, they will drop your sentence to how low?"

"Twelve years," Gallon said calmly, not at all intimidated by Ober's thinly veiled innuendo.

"So it's very important for you to please the State Attorney's office, isn't it?"

"To tell the truth."

"Pardon?"

"They don't want me to lie," Gallon said in a tone that implied he was correcting an error.

Ober stared long and hard at Gallon before finally letting out a contemptuously loud sniff, which let everyone in the courtroom know what he thought of Kenneth Gallon's credibility.

Even then, however, Gallon remained completely at ease, unaffected by Ober's dramatics before the jury.

70

The state's two most incriminating witnesses, Connie Beasley and Kenneth Gallon, both seemed entirely credible on the witness stand. Credible, that is, in the view of the prosecution team. It was always a mistake to assume that a jury would perceive things the same way. And besides, Skye knew that come time for closing arguments, the defense would hammer away at both witnesses on the basis of their plea bargaining and self-interest in the matter. Skye knew that he needed a corroborating witness who had nothing to gain from what he said. And the investigators had found just such a witness in the person of David Barile.

A warehouse supervisor for All Points Distribution,

Barile knew Richard Anderson because of Anderson's frequent business calls to All Points on behalf of Tampa Forklift.

On the day of May 8, 1987, the day after Robert Grantham was killed, Anderson called on All Points Distribution. It was a slow day at All Points, and Barile and Anderson went into the break room to down a few beers and shoot the breeze.

After almost two hours of friendly chatter, Barile told the court, Anderson blurted something about being in trouble with the police.

A garrulous man who is not shy about asking direct questions, Barile asked about Anderson's troubles.

"I asked why or what, and he repeated he was in trouble with the police," Barile said under Skye's questioning. "He said he shot and killed a guy the day before."

"And how did you react?"

"Kind of shocked. I didn't . . . you know, I never had anybody tell me that before."

"Did he say anything else? Did you ask him anything else?"

Barile looked at Anderson sitting at the defense table, then back at Skye. "Well, you know, why would you shoot and kill somebody?"

"You asked him that?"

"Yes."

"What did he say?"

"For the money."

"What did he say about that?"

"Well, the guy, according to Richard, supposedly had a large sum of cash on him. As it turned out, he didn't have the money that Richard thought he had."

"Did he mention an amount that the victim did have?"

"Two, three thousand dollars."

"Was there any further conversation pertaining to the killing?"

"Yes. He said he shot the guy four times and then dumped his body in the woods. He also told me he had picked him up at the airport."

"What did you do after he told you all this?"

"Well, I didn't believe it. I told a couple of people what Richard said, and they didn't believe it either."

"Was one of the persons Larry Moyer?"

"Yes. And then I seen in the newspaper that Richard had been arrested, but I didn't feel that what he told me was going to add that much to it, and I really didn't want to get involved."

"So you never contacted the authorities?"

"No. Larry called me later and told me he talked to the police and had given my name to them. Then two officers got in touch with me. I remember one of them was named Steve Davenport."

When Mark Ober got his chance to question Barile, he concentrated on one thing.

"How was it that you knew Richard Anderson?"

"Through work."

"And did you know him to have a sense of humor?"

"Yes, sir."

"Joke around?"

"Yes."

"Did you take him seriously at everything he did or said?"

"No."

"And you mentioned that when you were talking you and Richard drank a few beers. How many did you have?"

"Five or so."

"And how many did Richard have?"

"Five or maybe six."

This time when Ober finished, John Skye told the court he wanted to question Barile again under re-direct.

"Now, you stated that in your association with Mr. Anderson he had a sense of humor, is that correct?"

"Correct."

"Now, when he was telling you these things, was he joking? Was he smiling?"

"No, sir. He had a worried look on his face."

"When he made the statements to you about killing someone, how many beers had you had?"

"Three, four."

"Did you feel that you were intoxicated?"

"No."

"Did he have a buzz on?"

"Not that I could tell."

Skye called former All Points Distribution employee Larry Moyer, a friend of both David Barile and Richard Anderson.

On an evening in early June, Moyer testified, he ran into Anderson at a store on Hillsborough Avenue. Kiddingly, Moyer said, "I heard you killed a guy."

"How did he respond?" Skye asked.

"He just said, 'We wasted a guy. We wasted a guy that was supposed to have a million dollars and he only had three thousand.' And I thought he was, you know, giving . . . just giving me some bull crap. I didn't think it was true."

"What happened at the end of the conversation?"

"Well, we dropped the subject and started talking about cars. He has a Buick turbo and I had a new Corvette. One thing led to another and we decided to drag. We raced down the road and then he went his way and I went on mine. Then I headed out of town for some professional races, and when I got back, my trucking manager told me that they had arrested Richard for murder. It was really hard for me to believe, but I got hold of Officer Hattan, who works the races at the fair grounds on Friday nights, and told him what Richard had said. Then two agents from the FDLE talked to me.''

When Skye's questioning ended, Fuente took over the cross-examination. Referring back to the June conversation between Moyer and Richard Anderson, Fuente asked, ''During that conversation, didn't he also tell you that Beasley killed Grantham and had set up the entire thing?''

''Can you tell me who Beasley is? I don't know who Beasley is.''

Fuente tried again. ''Let me repeat the question. Isn't it true that Mr. Anderson said that Beasley killed Grantham and set up the whole deal?''

''Is Beasley a man or a woman?''

Once more Fuente concentrated on his own question instead of the witness's confusion. ''Did he say that?'' Fuente demanded.

''I've never heard that name before,'' Moyer insisted.

And Fuente asked the same thing again.

''I can't answer that. I don't know Beasley. I've never heard the name before, and he certainly didn't say it.''

Some of the jurors were becoming visibly perturbed with Fuente's stubborn insistence on repeating the same line of questioning over and over again. Fuente, however, had very good reason for trying to extract the statement he wanted from Larry Moyer because, thanks to the discovery process in which the defense is entitled to advance knowledge of all prosecution interviews, Fuente knew there was something there to be brought out.

What Fuente never did realize during the course of his cross-examination, though, was that Moyer was not trying to be obstructive. He simply, and honestly, was not familiar with the name of Connie Beasley.

If Fuente had asked him about statements Richard Anderson made in reference not to Beasley but to his ''girlfriend,'' Larry Moyer's responses very likely would have been remarkably different than this confusion.

"Did you or did you not tell Deputy Hattan that Beasley had killed Grantham?" Fuente insisted to the last.

And, just as stubborn, Moyer insisted to the last that no such thing was said.

When Larry Moyer's testimony ended, John Skye stood and announced, "Your Honor, the State rests."

71

One of the most difficult decisions a defense attorney must make in a criminal case is whether to put the defendant on the witness stand in his or her own defense.

A defendant is not required to testify, and jurors are always instructed that no inferences may be drawn from a defendant's decision to remain silent.

Still, defense attorneys know that it is one thing to instruct a jury. It can be quite another to expect them to act in accordance with those instructions.

A jury that does not get to hear a defendant say in his own words that he, or she, is innocent will probably lean toward the prosecution's case.

Yet there are dangers inherent in putting a defendant on the stand. For example, since courtroom testimony does not lie within their area of expertise, they run the risk of convicting themselves. Not that they will openly and directly admit to criminal activity, but often, in their ignorance of the technical nuances of criminal law, they may allow a prosecutor to lead them into areas that open previously closed doors. A confession or piece of material evidence, for instance, may have been ruled ineligible for use as evidence—until or unless a defendant's errant tongue brings the subject up and inadvertently allows damaging evidence to be considered.

In Richard Anderson's case, however, William Fuente and Mark Ober believed Anderson himself would have to refute Connie Beasley's testimony if he were to have any chance at all to escape conviction and a very long prison sentence, or the death penalty. They called the defendant as their first witness.

"Tell us your name, please."

"Richard Harold Anderson."

"And what is your age, Mr. Anderson?"

"Thirty-nine."

"Are you married?"

"No, sir."

"Are you divorced?"

"Yes, sir."

"Do you have any children?"

"I have a son."

"What is his age?"

"Fifteen."

"Mr. Anderson, do you know Connie Beasley?"

"Yes, sir, I do."

"Would you tell this jury, please, when you came to know her and how?"

Anderson related the familiar story of shopping for a turbocharged Buick and ending up with the salesgirl as well as the car. They spent the night together following their first date, he said. And yes, there came a time afterward when she told him that she had been offered a large sum of money to sleep with Robert Grantham.

"I told her it just appeared to be an easy way to make some money to get her out of her situation of having to live at home with her folks. She could get her own place."

"Did you ever tell Ms. Beasley that you [yourself] would [have sex with] Bob Grantham for that kind of money?''

"Yes, sir.''

"Did you ever tell Ms. Beasley that you would kill him for that kind of money?''

"No,'' Anderson said, his voice and demeanor emphatic on that subject. He swore he never had.

Anderson went on to describe the afternoon of May 7, about how Connie had reached him by pager to tell him that Grantham was flying home that day, and about their meeting in Bartow and their drive to the airport in Orlando.

According to Anderson's version of the story, Connie intended to get Grantham's money up front and, presumably, sleep with him in exchange. She was to use Anderson's condominium in Tampa for the transaction, and Anderson would meet her there afterward.

He said he dropped Connie off at the airport gate and told her he would wait for her in the lounge in case she changed her mind. When she did not join him in a reasonable amount of time, he said, he left Orlando and drove Connie's Pontiac back to Tampa. There, he got a friend, a former girlfriend, to help him retrieve his own car from Bartow, then wasted time until he finally got a pager call from Connie telling him that it was safe to come home.

When he got there, he told the jury, he was confronted by a hysterical Connie Beasley waiting for him in the foyer.

Anderson told the jury Connie's words as he came in were, "I shot him. I think I killed him.''

72

"He's downstairs in the car," Connie told him.

Richard ran outside. Connie pointed out an older model Thunderbird, and Richard approached it. There he found an elderly man slumped in the driver's seat with blood dripping down his face.

"Connie, I'm going to call an ambulance."

"No, no, they'll take my babies. They'll take my babies. Please help me."

And so—or so Richard claimed—he did.

He said he drove to a wooded area off Williams Road and dumped the body, then returned to his condo where Connie showered and changed. He himself did not need to change, he said, because he saw no blood on his clothing.

Anderson also gave a rambling and nearly incoherent statement about why Connie shot Grantham, something to do with Grantham's insistence that they meet frequently for sex and threats about telling her father if she did not continue to see him.

"And she said she got really pissed off when he said that because she didn't want to have sex with the guy and he was rough with her. And, you know, I just said, 'Well, you know, what's done is done, and let's take his car and move it away from here.' "

Anderson recounted taking the car to the airport and trying to wipe away some of the blood. The purpose of it all, he claimed, was to protect Connie and her children.

Back at the condo Connie took another shower, he said, and this time he did strip and put his clothes into trash bags along with her clothing.

The gun, he said, was the one he kept at home—the one which Connie knew about—and that he now stored in his living room instead of the bathroom, where he usually kept it.

He said that he discarded the trash bags of bloody clothing in the dumpster for the apartment complex next door, and tossed the pistol off the 56th Street bridge.

When they returned home, he said, he did not eat as Connie had testified. And when he went upstairs he found a wad of currency on his bedroom dresser. He assumed that it was the money Grantham gave to Connie in exchange for sex, he said, and threw it into a drawer.

Both he and Connie were exhausted, he said, and soon went to bed. But to sleep only, not to have sex as Connie said in her sworn testimony.

The next day, Anderson claimed, he tried to work, but he ended up parking under a tree near the University of South Florida campus, where he sat and tried to think through the problems that now faced him and Connie Beasley.

Sniffling lightly as he related this part of his tale, Anderson told the jury, "I just sat there under a tree. I remember seeing about fifteen little school kids that were on, like, a field trip, going into the buildings. And I thought, man, I wish I could start over and be one of those little guys."

Prosecutor John Skye rolled his eyes. There was no way to tell if the jurors were buying Anderson's bathos.

73

Fuente asked Richard Anderson to tell the jury about his discussion with David Barile in the All Points Distribution break room.

"I think I'm in trouble," Richard told Barile.

"With what? Girls? Your job?"

"No, with the police."

"What happened? What's it about?"

"Somebody I know shot and killed some guy over some money and I helped hide him in the woods."

After talking with Barile, Anderson said, he got in his car and began aimlessly driving, wanting to be alone and sort things out. He drove for hours, and ended up, he said, in Savannah, Georgia. Although he had friends there and some relatives, he chose to remain by himself, although he did call Connie several times. Eventually he came home.

And when he returned home, Fuente asked, what was his relationship with Connie Beasley?

"It changed a lot. It just wasn't the same. She was talking about, you know, getting married and I just . . . I was seeing a couple of other women. When we first started dating, it was kind of fun, but now it wasn't the same."

Under Fuente's questioning Anderson recalled meeting Larry Moyer one afternoon and telling him that his girlfriend, not mentioning Connie Beasley by name, shot a fellow over money.

He remembered Connie's warning call, of course, and running to get away and being arrested. Later, in jail, he recalled seeing the news broadcast that was played in the courtroom earlier.

"I can't believe the bitch is doing this to me," he said at that time; or so he claimed in court.

And contrary to Kenneth Gallon's testimony, he also claimed he said nothing else to any other prisoner at that time.

"Mr. Anderson, did you shoot Robert Grantham?"

Anderson sat upright on the witness stand and squared his shoulders. Looking Fuente straight in the eye, he slowly and firmly stated, "No, sir. I did not."

Fuente and Ober called several additional defense witnesses in an attempt to discredit or at least cloud the prosecution's testimony.

But the testimony of Richard Anderson was in fact the heart and soul of his own defense.

After closing arguments by both sides, the case against Richard Anderson for first-degree murder would go before a jury of his peers.

74

After attorneys on both sides completed closing arguments and the judge had delivered his instructions, the jurors were given verdict forms and led by the bailiff to the room where they would deliberate Richard Anderson's fate. The time was 2:56 P.M.

Judge Graybill retired to his chambers, and the attorneys lounged in the hallway outside the courtroom, chatting amiably now that their combat was ended. Anderson was taken to a secure holding cell in the courthouse complex.

After an hour the jury sent a note out asking the judge what would happen if they could not reach a decision that day. Would they be allowed to go home and return tomorrow or would they have to stay overnight? And if they could not leave before five o'clock, would they be allowed to make telephone calls home to let their families know? The note was signed by jury foreman John Hardy.

The principals were brought back into the courtroom and the jurors were brought out for further instruction.

Judge Graybill told them that if they could not agree on a verdict that day, they would be sequestered for the night. If that were to happen, the clerk would notify their families by telephone. Each juror was allowed to give the clerk the phone number or numbers where notice was to be given, along with any messages or requests for personal items to be brought to them in the event of an overnight stay.

Shortly before 7 P.M. the foreman sent another note out that Graybill read to the attorneys and to Anderson. "Making progress. Can we have some light refreshments, i.e. coffee, doughnuts, soda, hot chocolate?"

The judge had the bailiff advise the jurors that a refreshment order could be provided but would take about an hour. They could also opt to break for supper and then retire for the night.

When the bailiff tried to deliver that message, he was turned away with a terse comment that the jury was in the midst of a vote. Minutes later another note came out.

"Unable to reach a decision. What is the latest we can stay?"

Again Graybill sent the bailiff in with a choice between refreshments or supper and retirement.

The next note was brief and to the point: "To hotel."

At 8:14 P.M. the bailiff escorted the jurors to the Hilton Hotel for the night.

Court reconvened the following morning at nine, and at 10:01 A.M. a final note was sent out by jury foreman Hardy.

A verdict had been reached.

The attorneys took their places, and Richard Anderson was brought into the courtroom again. Judge Graybill seated himself behind the bench, and the jurors filed into the courtroom.

Their demeanor was grim, and not one of them looked Richard Anderson in the face.

Judge Graybill asked the jury if they had a verdict, and the foreman announced that they did, handing a verdict form to the bailiff, who in turn handed it to the judge. The judge read the verdict in silence and gave the form back to the bailiff, who passed it to the clerk.

"Will the clerk please announce the verdict," Graybill ordered.

"We the jury," the clerk read in a loud, firm voice, "find in this cause as follows: The defendant Richard Harold Anderson is—" she paused—"guilty of first-degree murder. So say we all. Dated this eighth day of February, nineteen eighty-eight. Signed, John Hardy."

Richard Anderson looked straight ahead, displaying no emotion whatsoever. His lawyers, however, grimaced and slowly shook their heads.

On the other side of the room John Skye clenched his fists in a silent display of victorious emotion, and Lee Cannon grinned.

The judge announced that the penalty phase of the trial would begin immediately after lunch.

75

Under Florida law, the punishment for first-degree murder is either death or life imprisonment without possibility of parole for a minimum of twenty-five years.

Graybill explained this to the jury once they were back in session. He explained as well that while the final decision as to sentencing rests with the court, the jury must first decide on a recommendation as to the sentence they wish the court to impose. Additional evidence would now be presented to help inform the jury before they made their recommendation.

And under the penalty phase rules, unlike during the initial part of the trial process supplementary facts would now be fair game for the prosecution.

John Skye chose to call only one witness.

"Could you please state your name and occupation?"

"Scott Hopkins. I'm an investigator with the State Attorney's office in Pinellas County."

"Do you know Richard Anderson?"

"Yes, sir. I met him on July eleventh, nineteen seventy-three."

"And, Mr. Hopkins, did you have an occasion to arrest Mr. Anderson?"

"Yes, sir, I did."

"And did you have occasion later to be present in the courtroom when Mr. Anderson pled guilty?"

"Yes, sir, I did."

John Skye was leaning casually and seemingly quite comfortably relaxed against the podium, looking at the jurors and not at his witness. He knew the reaction the jurors would have when Hopkins spoke, and he quite frankly wanted the pleasure of seeing it for himself when it happened.

"What did Mr. Anderson plead guilty to?" Skye asked softly.

The jurors, perhaps catching onto some of Skye's anticipation, seemed rapt in the moment. Several of them were literally leaning forward as if to be closer to the moment.

"First-degree murder," Scott Hopkins answered.

If there had been any doubts about the guilty verdict contained within the jury box before that moment, none existed after it.

Under Skye's direction, Hopkins went on to tell the jurors about the murder of James Winans those years earlier, including the abandonment of Winans's car at Tampa International Airport.

"The State has no further witnesses, Your Honor," John Skye announced when Hopkins was done painting Richard Anderson as a multiple murderer before this jury.

The defense chose, at Anderson's direction, to present no witnesses.

Once again, if more briefly this time, attorneys on each side were allowed argument before the jury. John Skye asked for a recommendation of the death penalty. Mark Ober pleaded just as eloquently that his client be sentenced to life imprisonment.

And once again the jury of his peers retired to consider Richard Anderson's fate.

76

This time the jury required little time to reach their conclusion. Once again the jury filed into the courtroom and delivered the results of their deliberation to the judge for publication. Once more the clerk read aloud.

"A majority of the jury, by a vote of eleven to one, advises and recommends to the Court that it impose the death penalty upon Richard Harold Anderson."

The decision surprised no one in the room, although there were some groans of unhappiness from a group of spectators who had come in support of Anderson.

Judge Graybill thanked the jurors and dismissed them, then informed the remaining parties that sentencing would take place at 1:30 P.M. on Friday, February 16, 1988.

When that date arrived the attorneys were allowed again to present argument, largely mirroring their pleas before the jury earlier.

Anderson was invited to comment. He rose to his feet and, obviously nervous now despite his stoic demeanor throughout the trial, said, "I just maintain my innocence. I did not kill Robert Grantham."

Reading from a prepared text but also taking time to look up periodically at Anderson, Judge M. William Graybill intoned, "The defendant, Richard Harold Anderson, stands before the court convicted by the jury of murder in the first degree of Robert Grantham with the recommendation of eleven of the jurors that he be sentenced to death. After considering only the evidence before the jury, the court finds the following aggravating and mitigating circumstances.

"Statutory aggravating circumstances: One, the defendant has been convicted of another capital offense, to wit—the defendant, back in May of nineteen seventy-four, was convicted of murder in the first degree in Pinellas County, Florida.

"Two, the capital felony for which the defendant is to be sentenced was not only committed for pecuniary gain but was also committed in a cold, calculated, and premeditated manner, without any pretense of moral or legal justification. . . . The defendant, without any provocation whatsoever, shot the victim four times with a pistol . . . with which the defendant had obviously armed himself before getting into the victim's automobile with premeditated intent to murder and rob him. . . .

"Statutory mitigating circumstances"—the judge looked at Anderson—"none."

Anderson's Adam's apple bobbed nervously as he swallowed.

"Nonstatutory mitigating circumstances: The only nonstatutory mitigating circumstance established by the evidence is that the defendant's girlfriend, although an accomplice, was allowed to plead guilty to murder in the third degree of Robert Grantham for a maximum possible sentence of three years imprisonment.

"The Court also finds that the aforesaid statutory aggravating circumstances clearly outweigh the aforesaid mitigating circumstances to such an extent that the defendant should be sentenced to death as recommended by the jury."

Richard Anderson stood staring straight ahead. He acted as though he had not heard a word the judge said.

While the lawyers and a very few spectators looked on, two bailiffs led the defendant out the backdoor of the courtroom.

Within days he was transported to the Florida State Prison at Raiford, where he is now on death row.

Connie Beasley, who was represented by Jack T. Edmund of Alturas, Florida, arguably the finest criminal defense attorney in the state, could have received a maximum sentence of three years imprisonment under the terms of her plea bargain.

After meeting the conditions of her agreement and testifying for the state against her former paramour, Richard Anderson, she was sentenced to serve one year and one day in the Florida State Prison for Women.

She has since completed her sentence and been discharged from custody.

And Robert Grantham?

77

Robert Theist Grantham's disappearance set off the sequence of events that culminated in the arrests and convictions of both Richard Anderson and Connie Beasley.

But whatever happened to the missing man's body?

That has never been satisfactorily determined.

The Florida Department of Law Enforcement is convinced that Connie Beasley told the truth when she directed them to a wooded location off Williams Road between Buffalo Avenue and Broadway Avenue on Tampa's north side.

Richard Anderson, too, testified that this was where Grantham's body was discarded on the night of May 7, 1987.

The body was dumped there and so was Grantham's garment bag that he brought back with him on the plane from Las Vegas.

Yet when they searched for the body, nothing was found.

Even before Anderson was arrested, Ray Velboom and Steve Davenport were concerned with finding Grantham's body. After all, it is extremely rare for a first-degree murder conviction to be obtained when there is no body to prove that a murder has indeed occurred.

Before any arrests were made, before they had Beasley's cooperation, the FDLE agents had gone so far as to revisit the location where James Winans's body was located, and the separate Pinellas County site where Winans's skull was eventually recovered. They hoped that Anderson might have repeated his previous crime to the extent of disposing of Grantham's body in the same way and the same places that he had disposed of James Winans's corpse and head.

Later, using Beasley's directions, they conducted a search of the north Tampa area where Grantham's body should have been found.

A massive search was undertaken by all available FDLE personnel and additionally with the cooperation of some sixty Hillsborough County sheriff's deputies working on foot, by horseback, and with three-wheel motorized all-terrain vehicles.

Nothing was found either of the body or the garment bag.

A helicopter was called in to conduct a low-flying search, and, when that, too, failed, Special Agent Supervisor E. J. Picolo remembered a highly specialized canine team attached to the Connecticut State Police.

The dogs are specifically trained to search out human bodies. Their services are requested primarily in the wake of major disasters, when human remains may be buried under debris or inside wreckage.

At the FDLE's request, Connecticut sent dog handlers Troopers Andrew Rebmann and Kevin Rodino to assist in the search for Robert Grantham. The dogs found nothing.

Velboom and Davenport have come to believe that the only person who could tell them—Richard Anderson—will not.

Anderson's activities in the Grantham murder were markedly similar in many respects to those he displayed in the Winans murder. And the FDLE agents have come to believe that this very much included the disposal of the two dead men's bodies.

When Winans was killed, Anderson returned to the site without his accomplice's knowledge and removed the dead man's head.

This time, the agents believe, Anderson returned without Connie Beasley's knowledge and took away the whole body plus the garment bag.

But where did he take them?

Anderson testified that the day following the murder, he drove—aimlessly, he claimed—to Savannah, Georgia.

Thus, he could well have transported Robert Grantham's body and discarded it anywhere between Tampa and Savannah.

Between those two points there are Green Swamp, the great Okefenokee Swamp, and countless small swamps, sloughs, and bayous where, as jail inmate Kenneth Gallon claims Anderson suggested, alligators would have made short work of a human corpse.

Then too, Lyin' Bob Grantham was not the only party to the case who has been known to dissemble. When Richard Anderson said he was in Savannah, it is entirely possible that he was engaging in deliberate disinformation.

Claiming to have gone north, he could very well instead have taken Grantham's body south, where, along the desolate miles of the cross-state highway known as Alligator Alley, he could have dumped the body in the Everglades or its wild environs; there, or in any of the innumerable irrigation ditches, drainage canals, and water district ditches that cross and crisscross the wetlands of southern Florida.

Robert Grantham's body could be anywhere.

It has never been recovered.

Nor has the still missing garment bag that Anderson discarded the first time without bothering to prowl through its contents.

Robert Grantham came back from Las Vegas carrying only $2,600, which Richard Anderson and Connie Beasley found and subsequently spent.

But the man claimed in his telephone calls to have won much, much more than that. And there is nothing to say that ''they'' can't be after the paranoiac. Nothing to claim the liar must always lie.

Could Grantham have been carrying a large sum of currency in his luggage? Richard Anderson said nothing about that in court, nor did Connie Beasley apparently know anything about any more cash.

But could the tattered and weathered remains of Robert Grantham's garment bag still be lying in some muddy sink with thousands of dollars of cash molding and slowly disintegrating?

It is a question for which there seems to be no answer. Yet.

The Best in Biographies from Avon Books

IT'S ALWAYS SOMETHING
by Gilda Radner   71072-2/ $6.50 US/ $8.50 Can

RUSH!
by Michael Arkush   77539-5/ $4.99 US/ $5.99 Can

STILL TALKING
by Joan Rivers   71992-4/ $5.99 US/ $6.99 Can

I, TINA *by Tina Turner and Kurt Loder*
71570-2/ $5.99 US/ $7.99 Can

PATTY HEARST: HER OWN STORY
by Patricia Campbell Hearst with Alvin Moscow
70651-2/ $6.99 US/ $8.99 Can

SPIKE LEE
by Alex Patterson   76994-8/ $4.99 US/ $5.99 Can

OBSESSION: THE LIVES AND TIMES OF CALVIN KLEIN
by Steven Gaines and Sharon Churcher
72500-2/$5.99 US/$7.99 Can